The Convertible Girl

(New, Rewritten Version)

by **Daniel Simon**

SAMUEL FRENCH

FOUNDED 1830

New York Hollywood London Toronto

SAMUELFRENCH.COM

IMPORTANT BILLING AND CREDIT REQUIREMENTS

All producers of *THE CONVERTIBLE GIRL must* give credit to the Author of the Play in all programs distributed in connection with performances of the Play, and in all instances in which the title of the Play appears for the purposes of advertising, publicizing or otherwise exploiting the Play and / or a production. The name of the Author *must* appear on a separate line on which no other name appears, immediately following the title and *must* appear in size of type not less than fifty percent of the size of the title type.

CHARACTERS

CHRISTINA

In her mid-twenties, Christina is of Catholic heritage. The author has chosen her to be of Latin or Hispanic background, however, this is admittedly an arbitrary decision. She has been played at different times as Italian, as a German and as an Hispanic girl. In short, the character's last name need not remain "Fernandez" as indicated in the script, but can be a Donatelli, McGillicuddy, Swenson or whatever the look of the actress playing this role is most obvious to the audience. But the first name Christina must remain constant.

Christina is twenty-five years old in appearance and is a very attractive, sensitive albeit fiery person when aroused. In other words, she is half pussycat, half tigress. If there's anything that Chris wants most in life it is to be happily married with two or three or four or more children.

RON GOLDMAN

New York born, although living in Southern California in recent years, Ron is an attractive man in his mid to late forties. He has been divorced twice and his two children by his second wife are the apples of his eye. In fact, it is partly because Chris considers him the world's greatest father that she feels it is not enough for her just to love and live with him but to be married and have this man be the father of her children. Although outwardly a serious man, Ron has a great, innate sense of humor. In short, he is the kind of person who can alleviate pain sometimes by making jokes about his problems.

POLICEMAN (doubles as store delivery man)

A black man anywhere in his thirties or so. His main qualification other than the obvious ability to act, is to be physically strong enough to lift Ron and haul him around the room at a breakneck pace.

JONAS STEINBERG

A sensitive young man in his late twenties. A rabbinical student who also is athletic looking enough to be accepted as the basketball coach of the Jewish Community Center with which he is affiliated. He has a good, gentle sense of humor albeit, is not the kind of person who is "on" all the time.

DELIVERY MAN (doubles as policeman)

Black man in his thirties to forties. While not necessarily a man of erudition, he speaks without any trace whatever of a "street" accent.

RABBI SILVERMAN

In his fifties or sixties, a man who takes himself very seriously. When it comes to religion, he is all business. He has a perpetual stern look on his face but there is a reason for that—he has absolutely no sense of humor. He could be American-born, but if you choose to cast him as foreign-born, he should have little native accent remaining. Certainly he does not speak with the sing-song caricature style of speech, too often ascribed to cliche theatrical "rabbis." Though he is an orthodox rabbi, he is definitely NOT of the Chassidic sect, those who wear long coats and round square topped black hats. He wears a conservative dark business suit and fedora.

RABBI ROTHSCHILD

Like Silverman he, too, is an orthodox Rabbi, nevertheless, wears an American style business suit. When it comes to gentility and humor, he is the antithesis of Silverman. While genuinely religious, he doesn't stick to the book quite as zealously as does Silverman. He may be foreign born and while he does have a sense of humor, these laughs must be derived from his character as a sweet man, not because he speaks in any sing-song Yiddish speech pattern.

MRS. GOLDMAN

Picture the religious old Jewish lady Ron had led us to believe she was like. Got the picture? Now forget it and put all new film in your camera. The lady is the exact opposite of the woman Ron described earlier: American-born, thoroughly vital and fun-loving. A very up-to-date chic woman who carries herself with such assurance and verve, she completely belies her age of seventy-two. In short, a "Today" kind of woman.

RABBI HAHN

An authoritarian figure, albeit possessed of a sense of humor. Or, so he thinks anyway. He is used to having his own way because of his position as head of the synagogue—and enjoys making people wait on his every word and whim. A man with a deep, booming voice. He also wears a business suit.

TIME: Present

PLACE: Marina Del Rey, California

ACT I

Scene 1

SCENE: The Marina Del Rey, California townhouse apartment of RON GOLDMAN. It is after 2 a.m.

The entire play takes place on the lower floor which contains a living room, kitchen, dining room and a small guest bathroom. (With the exception of the bathroom, these can more accurately be called "areas" rather than "rooms."

The living area which takes up the entire Right side of the stage, is done in an eclectic combination of contemporary and traditional styling. Seen prominently is an end table upon which stand two telephones, one white and the other black. The door leading into the apartment from the street is on the UR side of the wall.

A stairwell, just right of UC, separates the living area at R from the kitchen area at UL. The stairs lead to the upper floor. Inside the stairwell is a small utility closet. On the wall at DSR is the guest bathroom. (The door opens IN at DS.)

On the US wall of the kitchen, there are some cupboards, one of which is practical. On the wall at L just DS and L of the kitchen is a sliding glass double door, through which we can see the patio and beyond that, a partial view of the marina and a small section of this condominium complex.

Separating the kitchen area from the dining area DS is a bar/counter. The two bar stools match the four low-backed chairs around the dining table.

Before the curtain rises, we hear a DOORBELL being rung constantly and insistently. Then we hear this noise interspersed with the caller's anxious POUNDING on the door at R. On this urgent note the play starts.

CHRIS'S VOICE. (*Offstage. Nearly frantic.*) Ron! It's ME, Chris! Open the door! ... Ron, darling, are you all right? ... Oh, God, please don't let me be too late!

(The curtain rises but the stage remains darkened except for a pencil thin stream of LIGHT coming in through the slightly parted curtains covering the patio door.)

CHRIS'S VOICE. Ron, I gave you back your key! I can't let myself in! Ron, please open the door! ... Hang on, darling, I sent for help! They're on the way!

(Now a pajama clad MALE FIGURE sleepily, no, groggily makes his way down the stairs in the semi-darkness. This is RON GOLDMAN, in his mid to late forties. Ron had taken sleeping pills only a short time before and the effects of the drug, as well as being awakened by the noise are evident intermittently throughout the entire scene. Before he reaches the bottom step, the BANGING and RINGING noises at the door stop. RON continues to the door, opens it. Then, seeing no one, HE closes the door and still in his semi-stupor, gropes his way up the stairs again. Now we see CHRIS who has run around the patio to the glass door. She wears a coat over her pajamas, has on bedroom slippers and appears to be in her mid twenties. SHE vainly tries to open the locked sliding glass door, then peers inside. Seeing no one, SHE bangs against the door, then looks around for something to throw against it. Having heard the noise, RON groggily comes down the stairs again,

opens the front door. Once more HE sees no one, closes the door and starts up again. Meanwhile, CHRIS has picked up a potted plant and prepares to throw it.)

CHRIS. Ron! I'm breaking down the glass! If you're still alive in there, stand back! (*SHE throws the plant against the glass door, it falls to the patio floor ineffectually.*) Goddam plastic containers!

(*Hearing the noise, RON turns and comes down the stairs again. This time HE turns L and heads sleepily toward the patio door. As CHRIS prepares to throw a wrought iron chair, SHE sees Ron in the room, heading toward her.*)

CHRIS. Ron, is that you? Oh, thank God, you're not dead any more!

(*RON opens the door. Immediately upon admittance, the greatly agitated girl enters and throws her arms around him.*)

CHRIS. Darling, when you called me, I got so scared—I tried to rush right over but my car wouldn't start and I couldn't get a taxi! Didn't the police get here yet? (*SHE turns on the LIGHT.*)
RON. (*Covering his pained eyes, turns LIGHT off with his free hand.*) P' lice?? Wha' p'lice?
CHRIS. (*Turns LIGHT on again.*) I called them right after I hung up!
RON. (*Turns LIGHT off again.*) Wha' the' hell ya call p'lice for?
CHRIS. (*In semi-darnkess.*) What do you mean, what did I—didn't you say you took an overdose of sleeping pills?

RON. Hunh! ... Oh! Yeah, sleepin' pills ... Can't think straigh' ... mus've been out cold. (*Reeling.*) Chris! I can't stay awake ...

CHRIS. (*Propping him up with one hand and turning LIGHT on with the other.*) NO! Ron, whatever you do, DON'T FALL ASLEEP!

(*Burdened by his weight, during following, SHE tries to walk him around. Continue this walking, carrying, stumbling, crying, etc. biz throughout following.*)

CHRIS. Keep walking, Ron! You've got to keep moving! ... Come on, Ron, stay on your feet! ... Up and at 'em, baby! ... Where are those goddam police? I took a *BUS*, I got here before THEY did!

(*Moving him along constantly, as THEY pass the dining table, SHE picks up an empty pill bottle.*)

CHRIS. Was this the bottle they were in, Ron? ... Answer me!!

RON. (*Squinting at bottle as HE is forced to keep moving.*) Hunh? ... Yeah ... thass the bottle—

CHRIS. Omigod! It's empty!

RON. Chris, I gotta lie down ...

CHRIS. (*Continually moving him along.*) How many pills were in there, Ron?

RON. H-h-how many??? ...

CHRIS. THINK! THINK! You've got to remember, Ron! How many pills did you take?

RON. Hunh? ... Ahmmm ... uh ... two, I took two pills.

CHRIS. (*Still hauling her heavy burden around.*) Okay, when the police get here, you tell them you took tw—

(For the first time SHE stops. RON has continued moving forward, now leans on her helplessly.)

CHRIS. TWO??? ... That's ALL??? ... You took only TWO pills???

RON. *(Eyes closed.)* Thass all. Wha' th' hell ya wakin' me up like a crazy lunatic?

CHRIS. *(Still stunned.)* When you called m—didn't you say you finished a WHOLE BOTTLE of sleeping pills?

RON. I did. I' been taking one every night but they di'n't work so tonigh' I finished th' last two 'n the bottle.

CHRIS. Omigod! *(Or Spanish epithet! SHE hurls him to the nearest chair.)* Like an idiot, I called the police to tell them you took TWO lousy— *(Furious.)* Do you have any idea how embarrassed I'm going to be when the police get here and see you're still alive??? *(Looks up.)* Please, Lord, I'll never ask for another favor again, just make me have given them the wrong address.

RON. *(Trying to separate eyelids.)* Hey! Don't fool around with God, I may need Him! I think my eyelids are stuck together! ... Chris! I can't keep my eyes open! They keep closing on me! ... Oh, God, now I can't keep them closed, either! Ogeez, I wunner if they teach Braille to people who can only blink?

CHRIS. What is that, supposed to be funny? I rush through the streets in my pajamas scared stiff I might get here too late and all you got to do is crack jokes?

RON. *(Eyes blinking away rapidly.)* I'm not trying to be funny. I wish I really was dead, I could use the rest.

CHRIS. *(Extending her trembling hands.)* Look at me! I'm still in shock! Did you ever see hands shaking like this?

RON. (*Trying to peer through quivering eyes.*) Looks like they're standing still. My eyelids must be going at the same speed.

(*THEY stand for a moment, her hands shaking and his eyes blinking.*)

CHRIS. (*Suddenly controls her anger.*) Okay, Ron. Now that you got me here in the middle of the night on a false alarm. I'll try to do whatever I can for you. (*Heading for door.*)
RON. Hey, really 'preciate tha', Chris ...
CHRIS. (*Opens door, pauses.*) I'm going out now to get you another bottle of sleeping pills. This time promise me you'll be more careful and take them all at once. (*Starts out again.*)
RON. Chris! Please don't leave me again! I've been half outta my mind since you walked out on me.
CHRIS. Things don't have to be that way, Ron—BUT—since that's the way you want them—hasta luego! (*At door, stops, turns, goes to white phone.*)
RON. Chris, please! All these weeks alone—never realized how empty my life was 'fore you came along.
CHRIS. (*Dials 411.*) Save that story for the police, Ron. They'll enjoy it much more than the one you're going to have to tell them, explaining why they're making an *emergency call* for a man who's having trouble falling asleep! (*Into phone.*) In Marina Del Rey. The Yellow Cab Company.
RON. Chris, didn't you miss me at all?
CHRIS. Aw, come on, Ron. You really think I can live with a man for a whole year and then put him out of my mind like he never existed? You want to hear me *say* it, is that what you want? ... Okay. ... I cried myself to sleep

every night. I buried my face in my pillow and I cried all night long.

RON. (*Moved.*) Oh, honey, did you really?

CHRIS. (*Tearfully.*) You know my expensive down pillows from Saks Fifth Avenue? I had to throw them out because the feathers got all soggy and they stunk up the room.

RON. If you loved me so much, why did you move out? Chris, I swear, I don't understand you.

CHRIS. That's why I moved out. (*Into phone.*) Thank you. (*Hangs up, redials.*)

RON. We were happy together for a whole year! Why the hell was it so important all of a sudden for you to be *married*?

CHRIS. You call that HAPPY, the life I had to lead? What kind of existence is that for a woman? Every weekend when you have your children over, I have to move out so they shouldn't know we're living together! Comes every Friday night, I have to pack all my clothes and move in with my girl friend Doris in Santa Monica! Sunday nights, after you bring your children back to their mother in Encino, I have to pack once more and move back in here again! Hey, I'm sorry, Ron, I can't stand all that PACKING and UNPACKING, MOVING IN and MOVING OUT every weekend! Find someone who can handle that kind of life! See if you can get a driver from the United Van company to come live with you!

RON. (*Drowsiness getting heavier.*) Chris, I'm too tired to argue tonight ...

CHRIS. Then go back to sleep. If you dream abut a wedding, call me. (*Into phone.*) Hello. Will you please send a cab to 14000 Tahiti Way ... Thanks. I'll be waiting outside. (*Hangs up, starts for door.*)

RON. WILL YOU WAIT A GODDAM MIN—Oh, geez, I think I shook the blood vessels outta my eyes ...

Okay, okay, Chris, tell me how can I marry you with all that alimony and child support payments hanging over my head?

CHRIS. Aw, Ron, what makes you think it's cheaper for you if we only LIVE together? I eat just as much single as I do married. ... Agh, if it's not one alibi with you, it's another.

RON. What about the sixteen years difference in our ages? Doesn't that bother you?

CHRIS. What's sixteen years? There was nineteen years difference between my Aunt Carlotta and my Uncle Pedro.

RON. They got divorced, didn't they?

CHRIS. That had nothing to do with her being nineteen years older than him.

RON. What about my health? Doesn't it bother you that I have all the old men's ailments: a lousy prostate condition, bursitis in my arm that—

CHRIS. Ron, don't you understand I love you? Those things don't bother me. I don't even care about your bad back.

RON. I wouldn't care about my bad back either, if I had a good front.

CHRIS. That's it! That's the last excuse I ever want to hear! If it's not the difference in our ages, it's the difference in our health. If it's not the difference in our health, it's the difference in our backgrounds. If it's not the diff— Hey! I just thought of an excuse for not marrying me, you haven't thought of yet: There's a difference in our sexes!

RON. Why can't you un'erstand these're all legitimate problems we'll have to face sooner or later?

CHRIS. Why do you keep fighting this? Why can't you see how much you miss being married?

RON. I miss being married? Are you kidd— Name me ONE thing I miss in not being married.

CHRIS. Oh, now you're really asking for it. Okay—you're such a loving father, there's nothing more you'd love than having your children live with you *all the time!* Not just on *weekends* like you have them now but to SEE them and BE with them *every* MORNING and *every* NIGHT! You're a man who loves having company over for dinner but you want someone else to cook and serve and clean up after. You love being nursed when you're sick. You love being nursed when you're not sick. You hate to go to bed at night alone. You hate to wake up in the morning alone. Okay?

RON. Okay. That's ONE thing, what else?

CHRIS. HOW CAN YOU BE SO STUBB—? How many times did you tell me this was the happiest year of your life?

RON. It was. Before you came along. I had no life without you. Remember when you met me, right after my second divorce, the terrible shape I was in?

CHRIS. I remember, Ron. You were trying to hop in the sack with every bimbo in town. That's why I considered myself the luckiest woman in the world.

RON. For meeting me?

CHRIS. For not CATCHING anything from you! (*Heads for door again.*)

RON. Chris, please don't go. I'm miserable without you around.

CHRIS Then why don't you admit there's not a logical reason left on earth why you shouldn't marry me and you're sweating bullets right now because you know that's true!

RON. You think you got it all figured out, it's that simple, right? ... Okay ... okay, you got an answer for this one? What am I going to do about my mother?

CHRIS. Your *mother*? What has *she* got to do with this?

RON. I couldn't possibly marry you as long as she's alive.

CHRIS. Why not? She'll love me once she meets me. I'm an adorable girl.

RON. You're an adorable GENTILE girl. My mother's a very religious Jewish lady. It would kill her if I married out of my faith. That's why she never comes here, 'cause she knows I've been living with you and by her strict religious standards, that's a terrible sin!

CHRIS. (*Shocked.*) Oh, wow! That's *really* hitting below the belt, Ron! Aw, come on, using religion as an excuse! We lived together over six months before you even *mentioned* you were Jewish.

RON. That's 'cause I always assumed you *knew!* What the hell'd you think I was with a name like Goldman, an Iroquois Indian?

CHRIS. Names don't mean a thing. How would I have known you were Jewish unless you told me?

RON. Does the Pope go all over Italy telling everyone he's Catholic? He ASSUMES everyone *knows!*

CHRIS. Wait a minute, hold it! If you have a mother who's so big on religion, how come *you* don't believe in God?

RON. Me? Who says I don't believe in God?

CHRIS. Yeah? How is it I never once heard you praying or anything like that?

RON. What the hell do you think I was doing all the time you were twelve days late? ... Okay, Chris, I admit I'm not the most religious man in the world but I certainly believe there's a God somewhere.

CHRIS. Not in THIS neighborhood!

RON. It's just that I'm not the kinda person who believes in going through all the *rituals* of religion like my mother does. She still lights candles every Friday night, goes to Synagogue, the whole religious bit. Well, God bless her, if that's what she believes in, I couldn't possible hurt her for the few years she has left. Don't you see, Chris, a woman like that would ... she could die if I did that to her.

CHRIS. .... Why didn't you tell me all this at the beginning?

RON. At the beginning when?

CHRIS. When we first started going together. I never would have come to live with you.

RON. (*Shocked.*) You wouldn't have lived with me because my mother is Jewish? I had no idea you were that bigoted!

CHRIS. (*Furious.*) I wouldn't have lived with you if I thought you had no intention of ever marrying me!! ... (*Pulling herself together.*) Okay, will you at least answer *this* honestly? Would you have married me if I *had* been Jewish?

RON. (*Feeling perfectly safe on those preposterous grounds.*) Of course I would. You know I love you.

CHRIS. Then tell you mother to call the caterers because I'm converting.

RON. (*Shocked, almost into full consciousness.*) ... You're WHAT???

CHRIS. I'm converting. I'm going to become Jewish.

RON. I took sleeping pills, what the hell kind did YOU take? ... What do you mean "you're going to become Jewish?" Just like that?

CHRIS. Don't worry, this is no snap decision. I've been toying with the idea for a long time.

RON. CONVERTING isn't the kind of idea you *toy* with! Taking up KARATE is the kind of idea you *toy* with! ... I don't want to discuss this any more, okay? The whole idea of ... of YOU becoming Jewish is — it's — it's utterly ridiculous!

CHRIS. Why? Lots of people have converted.

RON. Sure, but not—not someone like you. You're the worst Jewish prospect since Sammy Davis, Jr.

CHRIS. What's wrong with me?

RON. There's nothing wrong with you, it's just that I—I simply can't conceive of YOU being Jewish! You're the most typical shicksa I ever saw.

CHRIS. What's a shiska? (*Sic*)

RON. You want to convert and you have to ask, "What's a shicksa?"

CHRIS. If I knew what a shiska is, I wouldn't have to convert

RON. A shicksa is a Gentile girl. And it's not "shiska," it's shicksa. You never heard of the word "shicksa"?

CHRIS. No, I only heard of "shiska."

RON. What the hell kinda word is "shiska"?

CHRIS. You never heard of "shiskabob"?

RON. (*Stares at her a long moment.*) ... Aw, come on, Chris, this is all a put-on, right? ... Wait a minute! Hold it! Those pills DID work and this is all a dream! Thank God! At last I'm getting some sleep! (*Lies head down.*)

CHRIS. Why is this so hard for you to believe?

RON. (*Disappointed that he isn't sleeping, raises head again.*) Because converting isn't something simple and easy like going to a store to buy a new dress or hat. Chris, you can't take home being Jewish for a few days and then bring it back to exchange if you decide it doesn't look good on you. You can't even change it for another COLOR.

CHRIS. I'm not exchanging one religion for another. I've never been really religious, anyway. Maybe that's what I've been missing in my life? I need something more to hold on to, something to believe in. Ron, lots of people are turning to religion these days. Ron, I believe this is something I really NEED!

RON. But are YOU something my MOTHER needs? ... Oboy, this isn't the best idea I ever heard, Chris—CHRIS! What a name for a Jewish girl!

CHRIS. The more I think of the whole idea, the more I like it. Hey, you want to make your mother real happy? We'll get married in a Jewish church.

RON. That'll be her biggest thrill. We'll hold the ceremony in Saint Anthony's Synagogue ... What about YOUR mother?

CHRIS. No, I don't think she'll want to convert.

RON. Just tell me how that sweet little Hispanic lady is going to react to this little news, hah? She'll go right into hysterics. She'll probably put one of her special Latino curses on me.

CHRIS. Hey, my mother's not that kind of person and you know it.

RON. She's not, huh? Remember how she carried on when you told her you were even *dating* me? I'm telling you, she'll put such a curse on me—*THAT'S* where my prostate condition came from!

CHRIS. My mother'll ignore the whole thing. She's not religious and the only thing she cares about is my happiness. So that takes care of your last excuse. Ron Goldman, you're a dead pigeon.

RON. (*Sleepiness returns stronger than ever.*) Chris, I ... I can't stay awake any more. I can't function unless I get at least eight hours sleep every month ... Okay, you win. You'll move back in here with me ... and after you convert and become Jewish, we'll get married and I can get some sleep.

CHRIS. Oh, darling, you just made yourself the happiest man in the world! (*Kisses him, heads for door.*) I'd better go home and get my things together if I'm moving back in tomorrow. I don't want to go out in the morning dressed like this.

(*We hear the sound of a CAR MOTOR from the patio.*)

CHRIS. I hope that's my taxi! (*Runs to patio, opens door, looks out.*) It is! (*Calls out.*) Taxi!

(*Sound of CAR STOPPING quickly.*)

CHRIS. Hey, is that a great omen? Everything lucky is starting to happen already. (*Shouts to Cabbie.*) Hold it, I'll be right out! (*To Ron.*) Goodnight, sweetheart, sleep tight! (*Blows him a kiss, starts through patio door.*)
RON. (*Sleep starting to overcome him, rouses himself to call out:*) Chris!
CHRIS. (*Stops, turns.*) Yeh?
RON. This means a tremendous change in your life. Are you really SURE you want to convert?
CHRIS. Why? Now you got some problems marrying a Jewish girl?

(*The taxi driver blows his HORN impatiently.*)

CHRIS. See you tomorrow, darling! (*SHE rushes out, leaving the patio door open.*)
RON. (*Exhaustion overtaking him again, calls out sleepily.*) The light! You forgot to turn off the li—

(*HE gets up, staggers toward the wall switch and turns it off, starting to fall asleep on his feet, slowly sinking to the floor. Offstage we hear the sound of the TAXI driving off. RON turns to head for the stairs, just about losing consciousness, realizing he can't make it up the stairs, falls asleep on the sofa.*
From outside we hear the sound of a SIREN and see the flashing RED LIGHTS of a police car. Then

FOOTSTEPS are heard coming up the front steps. We hear KNOCKING at the door. Then silence and we hear the sound of RUNNING FEET. Then we see the form of a POLICEMAN at the patio door. HE sees it is open and enters, turning on his search LIGHT. HE spots Ron lying on the sofa, first noticing the empty pill bottle on the table.)

POLICEMAN. Holy shit! He took the whole bottle! (*HE checks out Ron's heart beat, then takes a two-way radio out of his pocket, speaks into it.*) Hello, Smitty? That call was on the level! Get Emergency, we'll have to pump his stomach out!

(*HE yanks the sleeping RON to his feet, then has him walking around the room—no, running around the room twice as fast as Chris was able to do.*)

RON. (*Being manhandled around the room at a mile a second clip, tries to call out.*) I only took TWO pills! I swear thass all I took—

(*And on this frenetic action we fade the LIGHTS very fast and bring down the CURTAIN.*)

Act I

Scene 2

The same set. Several days later, late afternoon. In the kitchen, CHRIS, in a casual pants outfit, is pouring coffee into a glass. DSL, a young MAN in his late twenties is admiring the view of the marina through the patio window at L, made possible because the curtains are now parted wider.

The young man's name is JONAS STEINBERG. He wears denim pants, sneakers, a turtleneck pullover sweater and a two-colored satin basketball jacket. He wears a yarmulke (skullcap) on his head. When HE turns, we will see stenciled on the back of his jacket: "Santa Monica Hebrew School Wildcats."

[NOTE: From time to time, we hear the sounds of BOAT WHISTLES from boats in the marina.]

CHRIS. (*Bringing coffee to him.*) Here you are, Rabbi Steinberg, a hot cup of coffee. In a glass, right?

STEINBERG. Thank you, Miss Fernandez.

CHRIS. (*As HE takes a sip.*) Are you sure you wouldn't rather have a cup of coffee in a *cup?*

STEINBERG. Miss Fernandez, I taught you that in your first lesson: I'm not allowed to drink from a cup in a non-kosher home.

CHRIS. Oh, yeah, right, I keep forgetting .. Uh, I'm sorry, why not, again?

STEINBERG. (*Patiently.*) Because a cup is considered part of dishware and all your dishes are trayf.

CHRIS. Trayf? ... Trayf? ... Ahm, wait a minute, I should remember what trayf means? ...

STEINBERG. (*It's not easy to remain this patient.*) Whatever's not kosher is trayf. An orthodox Jew cannot eat or drink from dishes in a non-kosher home, Miss Fernandez. And your apartment is not kosher.

CHRIS. Oh, yeah. I'm sorry about that. When we moved in, the landlord never told us that.

STEINBERG. (*How much more can he stand?*) Miss Fernandez, apartments aren't built *already* kosher! You have to MAKE them kosher!

CHRIS. (*Puzzled.*) Oh, right, right.... Uh ... how do I do that?

STEINBERG. It's a whole megilleh. You have to buy meat only from a kosher butcher. You have to get rid of all your old pots and pans as well as all your dishes and silverware, and buy all new things to cook and serve with. You have to—

CHRIS. What's wrong with the things we have now?

STEINBERG. You've already mixed up the meat with the dairy. A kosher housekeeper must keep everything separate. You can't cook or serve meat in things in which you've already used for dairy dishes. And you can't cook or serve dairy in things you've already used for meat.

CHRIS. Why? Does it kill the taste? ... When you cook with a Chinese wok they say to blend everything togeth—

STEINBERG. FORGET A CHINESE WOK! This is the Law of Kashruth—Kosher! How many times do we have to go over the same ground, Miss Fernandez?

CHRIS. (*Setting coaster on table.*) Rabbi Steinberg, I'm a little nervous. You think maybe it'd help me relax if we made it less formal? How about if we called each other by our first names?

STEINBERG. Whatever works best for you.

CHRIS. Great. You call me Christina and I'll call you rabbi.

STEINBERG. I'm not a full rabbi yet, I'm still only a teacher. So if it'll make you feel more comfortable, why don't you just call me Jonas.

CHRIS. (*Picks up book.*) No, I think I'd better call you Rabbi. If I don't, it could be real embarrassing later on.

STEINBERG. Why?

CHRIS. Well, if we got so personal now, it might be hard for me to be that honest some day when I come to you for confession. (*Looks for place in book.l*)

STEINBERG. (*Wonders, is she serious?*) ... Don't you know Jews don't have confession?

CHRIS. (*Looks up.*) Ohh ... Then ... well, when Jewish people have very personal problems they want to talk over in private, who do they go to?

STEINBERG. (*Who else.*) *EVERYBODY!*

CHRIS. (*Thinks about that a long moment.*) Isn't that funny? I always thought every religion had *some* kind of confession.

STEINBERG. Actually, we do have something similar. Only we don't call it confession. We call it Complaining.

CHRIS. (*Smiles.*) You know, I'm beginning to feel more comfortable with you. Maybe I will call you by your first name, Johnny.

STEINBERG. (*Uncomfortably.*) Not "Johnny," please. Jonas. There are no rabbis named Johnny.

CHRIS. What's wrong with Johnny? John is a name from the Bible.

STEINBERG. Look, we Jews have an agreement with the Catholics. We don't name any rabbis Johnny and they don't name any priests Seymour ... May we continue, please.

CHRIS. (*Leafing through book again.*) Sure.

STEINBERG. Now ... What is one of the most important lessons a Jewish housewife must remember in the keeping of a kosher home? ... Without the book, please.

CHRIS. You'll be much happier hearing me say it WITH the book.

STEINBERG. From memory, please.

CHRIS. (*Reluctantly closes book.*) Ahmm ... I know it has to do with keeping some dishes separate from each other, right?

STEINBERG. (*Trying to be patient, nods.*) What are the two different kinds of dishes you have to keep separate from each other?

CHRIS. ... The cups from the saucers?

STEINBERG. (*Reacts, a bit exasperated.*) The MEAT from the DAIRY!

CHRIS. You're right.

STEINBERG. *I* know I'm right! This is YOUR lesson, not MINE!

CHRIS. I'm sorry, there's so much to learn.

STEINBERG. (*Losing some of his enthusiasm.*) I don't suppose there's any use asking you the Jewish names for the meat and dairy courses?

CHRIS. Oh, sure. I remember those. The meat course is called "Fleshy Dickey" and the dairy is called—

STEINBERG. (*Trying to control himself.*) Fleshy Dicky ... (*Gets up, walks away.*) Please, not "fleshy dicky." (*Enunciates carefully.*) Flayshuh dickuh.

CHRIS. Flashuh—

STEINBERG. Flaysh! Not flash, *flaysh!*

CHRIS. Flaysh.

STEINBERG. Uh!

CHRIS. Uh.

STEINBERG. Dickuh.

CHRIS. Dickey.

STEINBERG. *UH!* Dick-*UH!*

CHRIS. (*Carefully.*) Dick-*UH.*

STEINBERG. All together: Flay-shuh Dick-uh.

CHRIS. Flay-shuh Dick-uh.

STEINBERG. (*Encouraged.*) GOOD! ... Now! ... What are the diary dishes called?

CHRIS. Milkey dickey.

STEINBERG. (*Despairingly.*) Milky dickey ... (*Losing some control.*) MILCHUH DICKUH!!! ... What milky dickey? ... You make it sound like a candy bar!

CHRIS. (*Testing sound on tongue.*) Milch—millich—gee, that "chuh" sound is tough to get.

STEINBERG. The "chuh" isn't that important, it's the "dicky" that's driving me crazy!

CHRIS. I'm sorry. It's hard to remember so many things. You must keep the meat dishes separate from the dairy dishes. You have to keep the Passover dishes SEPARATE FROM THE REST OF THE YEAR. You mustn't CUT or TEAR PAPER on the Sabbath. You mustn't RIDE or WRITE or HAVE THE LIGHTS ON during the Sabbath. You mustn't—

STEINBERG. You CAN have the lights on! You mustn't TURN them on during the Sabbath!

CHRIS. How can you *have* them on if you don't TURN them on?

STEINBERG. You must turn them on *Friday afternoon* BEFORE the Sabbath starts in the evening. BEFORE the sun goes down.

CHRIS. What if you forget to do that?

STEINBERG. Then you must leave them OFF! ... *or* ... you can have a Gentile turn them on FOR you! ... Only you must make that arrangement BEFORE the Sabbath! ... And if you forget to arrange that BEFOREHAND, then you're not allowed to ASK a Gentile to do it for you.

CHRIS. (*Rises, walk away from table.*) Oh, wow, this is a lot more complicated than I thought if would be.

STEINBERG. Who said it would be easy? If we made it *too* simple, half the Arabs would want to become Jewish.

CHRIS. Millich—michel—

STEINBERG. Forget the pronunciation. I'm more concerned that you grasp the full significance of our customs and traditions.

(*HE motions for her to sit again, SHE goes back to table.*)

STEINBERG. Okay. Do you remember what a mezzuzzeh is?

CHRIS. A muzzumzeh—muzzezzum—

STEINBERG. A mezzuzzeh. I taught you that last week.

CHRIS. M–muzzumze—yes. I can't pronounce it but I remember what it is.

STEINBERG. Good. Then tell me, why do we hang a mezzuzzeh outside the door and kiss it every time we leave or enter?

CHRIS. (*Chagrined.*) Agh! I must have that wrong. I thought you were talking about that hard bread.

STEINBERG. THAT'S MATZOH!!! (*Wearily.*) Christina, tell me ... have you given any serious thought to some other religion BESIDES Judaism?

CHRIS. Rabbi, I HAVE to become Jewish! I told you that.

STEINBERG. And I told you when we first started, if the only reason you're converting is because you HAVE to, then please forget it. A Gentile can be converted *only* because he or she WANTS to be.

CHRIS. I DO want to be.

STEINBERG. For no other reason than to embrace the faith?

CHRIS. Yes.

STEINBERG. Not just to get married?

CHRIS. No. (*Super innocently.*) It's just the *wildest coincidence.*) that the mother of the man I'm going to marry will throw herself off the roof if I don't become Jewish.

STEINBERG. Okay. Talking to ME like that is one thing. But remember, you're going to take your final test before three rabbis. Try shticks like that on them and William F. Buckley would stand more chance than you of becoming Jewish.

CHRIS. I'll be careful.

STEINBERG. By the way, you'll have to pick yourself a new Jewish name. *Christina* doesn't quite cut it for us.

CHRIS. Ohh ... What do you think about Maria Theresa?

STEINBERG. Why? You planning to become the first Jewish nun?

CHRIS. How about taking my mother's name, Pepita Conchita Rosario?

STEINBERG. Forget it. Here, you can borrow this book. (*Hands her a book.*) Pick out a name like Esther or Shirley or Muriel. Any of those names will prevent cardiac arrest.

CHRIS. (*Laughs.*) You have a great sense of humor. That's what I like about Ron, too.

STEINBERG. Ron? What is that. some kind of new religion like Zen?

CHRIS. Ron is the man I'm converting fo—this fellow I'm involved with. You make me laugh the way he does. I think a sense of humor is the most important quality a person can have—next to a great love for children.

STEINBERG. (*Touched by her sincerity.*) Christina, no student I've ever taught has tried harder than you ... but, are you absolutely sure converting is for you? I mean, it would give me a terrific thrill to say that a girl with your face and figure is Jewish but—taking a step like this isn't for everyone.

CHRIS. Rabbi, no offense but personally I don't think it's that important to be Jewish OR Gentile. I don't come from a very religious family. My father was originally Catholic but he gave that up to marry my mother who was a Christian Scientist. Her mother was a Jehovah's Witness and her father was a Seventh Day Adventist—for five or six days. So, no one knows what I'm converting FROM.... Why? You thinking of flunking me?

STEINBERG. It's not up to me to flunk you or pass you. I just want to be sure you understand all the difficulties of keeping a kosher home—and dedicating your whole mind and soul to the keeping up of every one of our Holy Laws and traditions and customs. It's something you must be willing to do every single day.

CHRIS. You mean I have to keep that up for a whole year?

STEINBERG. For your whole LIFE. No days off ever. Some women find it absolutely impossible to keep up and quit in frustration after the first few weeks. It's even difficult to keep up for women who were *born* Jewish.

CHRIS. Really? I always thought all Jewish women kept kosher homes.

STEINBERG. Would you believe, in this whole town, the most kosher girl I've met so far is YOU. (*Glances at watch.*) Say! It's getting late! I better get going if I'm going to make the Friday night services.

CHRIS. Friday night!? I forgot! What time is it?

STEINBERG. (*Gathering up his books.*) Almost five o'clock.

CHRIS. Five o—Holy Mother of Jesus!

(*This outburst so startles the young man that HE drops his books crashing to the table. At the same time, CHRISTINA has dashed to the utility closet from which SHE takes out two suitcases.*)

CHRIS. Excuse me, Rabbi, I have to pack!

STEINBERG. (*Gathering up books again.*) Oh? You going away on a trip?

CHRIS. (*Running up the stairs.*) No, I'll be in town. I always move out every Friday night.

STEINBERG. I don't understand. If you live here, why do you always move out every Fri—?

(*His question remains unfinished and unanswered since Chris is out of earshot anyway. As HE puts his books into his attaché case, the front door opens and RON enters, carrying several large paper bags filled with groceries.*)

RON. Oh, hi. You must be the teacher Chris is studying with. (*On his way to kitchen, passes Steinberg notes the basketball jacket.*) You converting the Lakers, too?

STEINBERG. Hunh? Oh, I was just coaching the basketball team at the Community Center before I came here to give your daughter her lesson, Mr. Fernandez.

RON. (*Setting bags on counter, reacts.*) My name isn't Fernandez. It's Goldman, *RON* Goldman.

STEINBERG. (*Embarrassed.*) Oh!! Then YOU'RE the one who—

RON. That's right. I'm the one who's engaged to my daughter.

STEINBERG. Oh, look! I'm very sorry. I hope I haven't embarrassed you.

RON. Forget it. I get that from everyone. I'm losing my hair so people assume I'm old enough to be her father.

STEINBERG. I assure you, I didn't think that at all.

RON. I'm glad because I'm two years older than her father. (*Starts to store things in pantry and refrigerator.*)

STEINBERG. You need any help with that?

RON. Oh, thank you.

(*During the following dialogue, STEINBERG will help RON store things away.*)

RON. I have to stock up for the weekend because my kids are coming over.

STEINBERG. You have children? And you're bringing them HERE?

RON. Sure. They stay with me every weekend. Why?

STEINBERG. Well ... obviously you and Christina are—are— (*Hesitant to mention it.*)—I mean, don't you consider it a bit embarrassing for your children to see you ... *living* with someone who's not your wife?

RON. They SAW me living with my wife and THAT embarrassed them even *more*. (*More seriously.*) No, actually, I DON'T want my kids to see it. That's why I think it's best for Chris to move out every weekend when I have the kids over.

STEINBERG. Oh! THAT'S what she meant when she—I must say, Mr. Goldman, in these times most people would consider that a rather—well, *dated* attitude. I mean, today most people don't seem to worry that much about conventions. It's nice to still find someone around with your old-fashioned sense of morality.

RON. Oh, plenty of people feel the same way I do. Especially when it comes to their children. It's just that ... I feel it's my parental obligation to protect my kids' sense of values about sex until they're old enough to deal with situations like this. They're confused enough about marriage as it is. (*RON now puts emptied bags on the bar/counter and folds each one neatly.*)

STEINBERG. Confused? You mean because you're divorced?

RON. It's not just *divorced*—it's that my ex-wife is— look I'm embarrassed to say something like this to a person in your position—okay, my ex-wife is—*carrying* on with some college boy who—

STEINBERG. What do you mean, "carrying on"?

RON. You know ... "carrying on." I'm sorry, I find it hard to use more graphic language talking to a rabbi.

STEINBERG. I'm not a rabbi yet. I'm still only a teacher.

RON. Oh. She's screwing this kid.

STEINBERG. (*Uncomfortable.*) So! Your ex-wife and this boy are "carrying on" together. How old a woman is she?

RON. Thirty-nine, forty, I can't remember. Anyway, she and her kid—

STEINBERG. How did a woman that age get involved with such a young boy?

RON. I think it was at a PTA meeting. *She* was there with OUR kids and *he* was there with HIS mother and father! It's a joke! It's a joke! I don't know where the hell she met him! (*Picks up folded bags, takes them to the cupboard, opens it to reveal it is stacked tightly with countless previously folded bags, forces new bags in somehow, with STEINBERG's help.*) What gets me is she's feeding him on MY alimony! He probably uses the money he saves on food to pay his tuition. Is that wild, I was married less than ten years and I'm sending a boy to college!

STEINBERG. How many children do you have?

RON. (*Picks up rag, starts cleaning around counter and elsewhere.*) Just two, a boy and a girl. Eleven and thirteen. Kids are incredible these days, the way they grow so fast. Can you imagine, eleven years old and already a head taller than me.

STEINBERG. That's pretty tall for an eleven year old boy.

RON. I'm talking about my daughter. (*Moves to stairwell, calls up.*) Chris! Are you ready yet? I've got to leave to pick up my kids!

CHRIS'S VOICE. (*Offstage.*) Didn't know you were home, darling! Be right down!

RON. (*Turns to Steinberg, more seriously.*) Rabbi, confidentially, do you think she'll really go through with this?

STEINBERG. It's too early to say yet. She's having a rough time so far but she's trying harder than any convert I've ever given lessons to.

RON. Suppose she does stick with it? How long do you think it'll take?

STEINBERG. All depends.

RON. On what?

STEINBERG. Whether she converts or I collapse from a nervous breakdown! ... Who knows? I've seen more impossible cases than her make it. And I've also seen some girls take instruction all the way through to the Mikvah and *then* quit.

RON. "Mikvah"? That's some kind of ceremony women go through when they convert, right?

STEINBERG. (*Nodding.*) A Mikvah is supposed to be the symbol of a new birth for a woman. Like whatever she was before, she's being born all over again, this time into Jewishness. So they cleanse the woman from head to toe of her old self. She is immersed completely in water. That's what Mikvah means: The Immersion.

RON. Oh. Well, where does this take place? In some Temple with a swimming pool?

STEINBERG. Mr. Goldman, the only Temple I know that has a swimming pool is SHIRLEY Temple.... You're supposed to use only natural water. Any place where water is piped in is considered unacceptable. And since there isn't any orthodox Mikvah in this area we're going to conduct Christina's ceremony in the ocean.

RON. In the ocean? I always thought women are naked in a Mikvah.

STEINBERG. In a regular Mikvah they are. And there's usually a woman supervising. But since we're going to the ocean, there'll be three rabbis there from the Synagogue to make sure her body is completely immersed in water, with absolutely no interruptions from any kind of clothing.

RON. You mean she's not allowed to wear any thing at all?

STEINBERG. Not a piece of jewelry, nothing. According to the *strict orthodox*, she must even take off her nail polish. However, *we're* not that rigid.

RON. Oh, good. I'd hate to see her become Jewish without nail polish. Okay, so Christina goes to the ocean and goes into the water naked. When does she become Jewish, before or after she's arrested?

STEINBERG. Mr.Goldman, believe me, there's nothing to worry about. She doesn't go *into* the water naked, she wears a muu-muu.

RON. A muu-muu! Ah! ... Why a muu-muu?

STEINBERG. Because a loose fitting gown like that will bubble up and float to the top. That way the rabbi and this two witnesses who are all watching from the beach can know that—

RON. Oh, the rabbis stay on the beach! They don't go in skinny dipping with her.

STEINBERG. Of course not. She's way out in the ocean alone. And when everyone sees the muu-muu float to the surface, they'll know for sure that she is now completely covered by water with NOTHING AT ALL over any part of her body! She's as bare as the day she was born.

RON. When the lifeguards see that, there could be the biggest MASS CONVERSION in history! ... Okay, then what happens?

STEINBERG. They say a prayer over her and that's it.

RON. That's the whole thing? You mean, then she's Jewish?

STEINBERG. It's not the WHOLE thing. She also has to go the Synagogue and pass the test by three rabbis.

CHRIS. (*Comes downstairs carrying two suitcases.*) Oh, you're still here, Rabbi?

STEINBERG. I was just leaving.

RON. (*Picks up her bags.*) Are you parked near here, Rabbi? Can I give you a lift to your car?

STEINBERG. Thanks, I have a motorcycle. I found a good spot just outside.

RON. Smart. The only way to find a parking space in this neighborhood is to have a motorcycle or be making it with a meter maid.

CHRIS. Ron! I don't think it's proper for you to be making dirty jokes in this house any more.

RON. Omigod! I created a monster! A Sadie Frankenstein! (*Starts for door.*) ... Come on, honey, I'll drop you off at Doris's house before I pick up my kids.

CHRIS. (*Starts to follow him, stops.*) Oh, no!

RON. What "Oh no!"?

CHRIS. I *can't* stay at Doris's this weekend! She has no room, her parents are visiting from Portland!

RON. (*Upset.*) Didn't you make any other arrangements?

CHRIS. I started to, then the rabbi came over and we got involved in my lesson and it completely slipped my mind.

RON. Oh, that's beautiful! Just terrific! My kids are coming over for the weekend and YOU have no place to stay! (*Nervously starts to pace.*) I KNEW something like this would happen some day! I KNEW those kids would find out about us one way or another!

CHRIS. Take it easy, Ron. They haven't found out anything yet. Until they can PROVE I'm living here, I'm still the Phantom Mistress.

RON. (*Pacing.*) Where can you stay this weekend? ... Where? ... (*HE inadvertently comes to Steinberg, stops and looks at the younger man intently, then back at Chris.*)

CHRIS. Forget it, Ron, he's not allowed to have anything trayf in his apartment.

RON. I didn't mean for you to stay with *him!* (*To Rabbi.*) I was wondering maybe *you* had some idea what we could do?

STEINBERG. Who, me? ... Well ... since you said you have them with you all the time, anyway—what if you took them away with you for the weekend and let Christina stay here this time?

RON. (*Excitedly, as HE sets bags down and goes to stairs.*) That's it! That's the answer! You're very good, Rabbi. I bet you're going to make it big some day and have your own chain of synagogues! (*Heading up stairs.*) I'll pack some things for myself, then I'll pick up the kids and take them to Disneyland.

CHRIS. (*Picks up her bags, also heads for stairs.*) I'll go up and unpack again.

(*On the way up, HE stops, turns, comes down, passing CHRIS coming up.*)

RON. I better call my kids first and tell them I'll be late! (*Heading for phone.*)

CHRIS. (*Stops on the stairs.*) Where am I going? I can stay at a hotel around here!

RON. (*Has already picked up black phone and dialled.*) A hotel! That's so simple, it never even entered my mind. (*Hangs up, then redials.*) I'll make a reservation for you.

CHRIS. (*Coming down again.*) Use my phone, honey. Keep yours clear in case your children call.

(*RON nods in agreement as HE puts down black phone, picks up white one, dials.*)

STEINBERG. You each have your own phones because of his children?

CHRIS. It was my idea. If I'm always picking up *his* phone, they'll suspect I live here.

STEINBERG. (*Admiringly.*) That's very clever. You've got a Yiddisher *kupp.* (*Pointing a finger to his head.*)

CHRIS. That's not my fault, I haven't had time to change the dishes yet.

STEINBERG. (*Reacts.*) No, that's a different kind of— (*Decides not to pursue it.*)

RON. (*Still waiting for phone reply.*) Hello? Have you got a single available for the weekend? ... Yes, I'll hold. (*To Chris.*) Can you imagine me using the wrong phone? How could I be so stupid?

CHRIS. You weren't stupid, honey. You were so concerned about your children, you got a little crazy for a minute. that's part of the reason I love you.

RON. (*To rabbi.*) You hear that. She loves me because I'm a kook.

CHRIS. Hey, you think squirrels are the only ones who love nuts?

STEINBERG. (*Looks at his watch.*) Well, it's getting late. I'm not allowed to ride after dark.

CHRIS. That's all right, it's safe around here. The streets are all lit up at night.

STEINBERG. I MEANT: religious jews aren't allowed to *ride* on the Sabbath and the Sabbath starts at sundown!

CHRIS. Oh, wow, am I ever going to get everything right? How do *you* keep track of so many different religious law and customs and traditions?

STEINBERG. Simple. I pin up little reminder notes on my refrigerator. Never mind, we'll review everything Monday.

CHRIS. Then you're not going to drop me?

STEINBERG. Drop you? I'm thinking of giving up two Bar Mitzvah students to make more time for you. (*HE waves goodbye and exits.*)

RON. ... That sounds fine, I'll take it. ... What? ... Oh, the name? ... Uh, Fernandez. *Christina* Fernandez. ... Yes, I've often been told I have an interesting voice for a girl. ... Yes, we'll be right there. (*Hangs up, picks up her bags.*) Let's go. You're set.

CHRIS. Wait a minute. Did I leave anything of mine behind?

RON. (*Impatiently.*) Will you hurry! My kids must be worried stiff. You know I'm never late to pick them up! Come on!

CHRIS. (*One last look.*) I think I've got everything.

RON. (*Has door open, indicating for Chris to hurry.*) Let's GO! My ex-wife'll kill me if I'm late tonight!

CHRIS. (*Heading for door, carrying bags.*) What's so special about tonight?

RON. (*Following her out.*) Her boyfriend's taking her to his PROM!

(*THEY exit as we BLACKOUT.*)

ACT I

Scene 3

Flash on screen, a picture of a crowded street in the Fairfax Avenue business district in Los Angeles, over which we hear the following dialogue on TAPE:
[Note: If screen is not practical, dialogue is heard in darkness:]
SOUND: A door opens, followed by the TINKLE of a bell. Then the SOUND of a woman's footsteps.

CHRIS'S VOICE. (*Offstage.*) I beg your pardon, sir. Is the store still open?

MAN'S VOICE. (*Dialect.*) Soitenly. Vot can I do for you, young lady?

CHRIS'S VOICE. Do you carry massagers?

MAN'S VOICE. Massagers? Vy shood I carry massagers in a store like dis?

CHRIS'S VOICE. I was told I could buy one here.

MAN'S VOICE. Dot's de funniest t'ing I ever heard. I voodn't dream of carrying massagers in a store like dis. Did you try de drug store down de street?

CHRIS'S VOICE. Yes. They said they don't carry them. When I described the kind of massager I was looking for, they said you probably carry them in here.

MAN'S VOICE. Dot's a complete mystery to me. Vy shood anybody told you I sell—vait a minute! Hold it just a second! Vot are you going to do mit dis massager?

CHRIS'S VOICE. My rabbi told me I needed one to hang outside my door.

MAN'S VOICE. A MEZZUZZEH!!

(*Bring up LIGHTS.*)

ACT I

Scene 4

*Same set. The following Friday. Chris has on a new outfit.
SHE is talking on the white phone at R. Her packed
suitcases stand near the front door. On the table are two
paper bags filled with such items as a new prayer book,
a candelabra, a number of candlesticks, a bottle of
Manischewitz wine, two glasses, a shawl, a yarmulke
(skull cap) and a loaf of choleh bread (a twist). These
will be seen only when she takes each out of bag and
sets them on the table.*

*It is important to note that as the scene progresses, the sun
will be descending and the room gradually gets
DARKER. However, the audience must NOT become
too aware of the gradual approach of nightfall. Start
dimming LIGHTS only when indicated.*

*During the following phone conversation CHRIS will
move to the dining table and take out items as needed.*

CHRIS. (*Impatiently.*) Hello? ... Oh, are you still
there? I was wondering what happened to you.... Yes, this
is Miss Fernandez.... I'm still waiting to find out what
happened to the dishes I ordered Monday, they should have
been here hours ago..... That's right, Fernandez. 14000
Tahiti Way, Marina Del Rey. (*More annoyed.*) Oh, please!
Don't give me that! Someone else just told me the truck
was on the way THREE hours ago.

(*The front door opens and RON enters, rotating one arm in
pain as HE carries in a supermarket bag filled with
regular supplies.*)

CHRIS. (*Covers mouthpiece, then to RON:*) Your bursitis again?

RON. (*In pain, nods.*) It came on right after lunch. I was feeling fine when out of a clear blue sky, I suddenly got hit by this stabbing pain in my—were you talking to your mother about me around two o'clock? (*Continues into kitchen to unload bags.*)

CHRIS. (*Into phone.*) That's right. I ordered three sets of dishes.... Yes, I'll hold.

RON. (*Having difficulty with his aching arm as HE unpacks.*) Did I hear you say you bought THREE sets of dishes?

CHRIS. (*Still on phone, nods to him as SHE takes candles out of bag.*) One set of milky dicky and one set of flesh—

RON. (*Laughing.*) Milky dicky! Every time you say that, it kills me—yoww! (*Laughter has caused further pain to arm.*)

CHRIS. (*Glares at him, continues.*)—and one set of fleshy dicky for every day and one set for company.

RON. (*Still in pain.*) Why kosher dishes for company?

CHRIS. A lot of our friends are Jewish, aren't they?

RON. So what? Only two of them are religious. And their idea of being religious is going to see a Barbra Streisand movie. (*Notices items on dining table.*) What's all that stuff for?

CHRIS. The rabbi wants me to practice my—(*Into phone before she finishes.*) Yes, I'm still here.... Ohh ... Well, if the truck's not here soon, he'll have to bring it back Monday.... No, I don't want delivery tomorrow. Tomorrow's Saturday and I don't do business on the Sabbath.

(RON reacts to that, heads for utility closet to take out heating pad which he will plug into electrical outlet, then bring it into living room to apply during following.)

CHRIS. As a matter of fact, if the driver doesn't get here soon, the Sabbath will be started and I can't accept it after sundown, either.

(RON reacts to that also.)

CHRIS. ... What? ... Yes, I did say my name was Fernandez. Hannah Fernandez.

RON. HANNAH? Why did you tell them your name is Hannah?

CHRIS. I told you last week, I had to take a new Jewish name.

RON. I thought you were kidding! ... I'm glad you didn't pick Bathsheba.

CHRIS. *(Into phone.)* No, I *can't* wait much longer. And I want you to know I think this is terrible.... If the truck isn't here before dark, they'll have to eat out of paper dishes all weekend on account of you people.... I hope so. Goodbye. *(Hangs up.)*

RON. What do you mean, we'll have to eat out of paper dishes? We have a perfectly good set of china.

CHRIS. Not any more we don't. I gave them away. *(Crosses to patio window, looks out.)* I hope that delivery truck gets here soon.

RON. You gave away my good dishes? The expensive set of Bavarian china my friends gave me for my divorce?

CHRIS. *(Still at window.)* They were trayf. You want me to do everything right, don't you?

RON. They cost a fortune! If I wanted to get rid of them, I could have sold them!

CHRIS. It's a blessing to give them to charity. I gave them to the Red Cross—but I didn't tell them the dishes were trayf. (*Leaves window, goes back to table, continues removing items from bag.*) What are you doing home from the office so early? You don't have to leave to pick up your children for an hour yet.

RON. I thought I'd put some heat on my arm before I left. Where's your teacher?

CHRIS. He's not coming on Fridays any more. The traffic's so heavy on the freeway, he can't get back to his synagogue before sundown.

RON. Too bad he's not a real rabbi yet. If he was, he could just do like Moses at the Dead Sea and all the other cars—(*Makes "parting of the sea" gesture with both hands as Moses might have created the original miracle.*)—would part and make a path for him—yoww!! (*The very end of the "parting" motion has caused great pain to his arm.*)

CHRIS. Serves you right. God just punished you for being sacrilegious.

RON. (*Rubbing his arm.*) I wasn't being sacrilegious. It was just a little joke. Don't you think God has a sense of humor?

CHRIS. God must have a terrific sense of humor. He was just sending you a warning sign of what He thinks of YOUR sense of humor.... Oh, I forgot to tell you to pick up plastic knives and forks for the weekend.

RON. What for? I took the kids on a picnic last week. What's wrong with using our regular silverwa—you gave *them* away, too?

CHRIS. (*Nods as SHE takes candles and holder out of bag, inserts candles into the holder.*) Along with the pots and pans. And a lot of food in the refrigerator had to go, too. I know what you're thinking: your mother's going to be very proud when she comes here, right?

RON. No, I'm thinking she's going to be very hungry.

CHRIS. (*Takes out prayer book.*) Would you please put on a hat.

RON. (*Applying heater to arm.*) My head's not cold. The bursitis is in my arm.

CHRIS. You have to keep your head covered while I practice my prayers. (*Takes yarmulke out of bag.*) Here's a YAMmakkeekee I bought for you.

RON. A YAMmak—a YARmulke!

CHRIS. They're very religious hats. The Pope wears one, too. (*Takes out shawl, puts it over her head, then picks up book and reads from it as SHE sings in authentic Hebrew air.*)

Boruch Atoh Adonoy

Elo-hanu Melech Ha-Olom

Ha Matzi Lechem Min Ho-oretz.

RON. What are you doing?

CHRIS. (*Sings following words in same religious chant so as not to break the somber spirit of the moment.*)

I'm doing my homework

The Rabbi wants me to practice

As much as I ca-a-an. (*SHE picks up a loaf of choleh bread and reads the following:*)

Blessed Art Thou, O Lord Our God

King of the Universe

Who brings forth the bread from the earth. Amen.

RON. Amen. Look, I—there's something I have to tell you ... because when I first mentioned about my mother being so relig—

CHRIS. (*Hasn't heard him because SHE has already started singing the following:*)

Asher Kid'shanu

B'Mitzvasov V'Tzivanu

El Chumatz O Matzoh. Amen. (*Puts down the bread.*)

RON. Amen. How did you learn how to Hebrew like that so fast? I studied for years and I can't read that good.

CHRIS. (*Picks up bottle of wine.*) I don't read it in Hebrew. I read it in English. It's spelled out phonetically. (*Opens bottle.*) I'm going to say the prayer for the wine now. You want to say it with me?

RON. I don't drink wine. See if they have one for Margueritas.

CHRIS. (*Angrily.*) I asked you to stop making bad taste jokes like that!

RON. Okay, I'm sorry! Boy, you really are taking this seriously, aren't you?

CHRIS. The more I study, the more I realize how important it is for people to hold on to their religion. Rabbi Steinberg said I'm picking it up real fast now. He said if I keep up this pace, I may be able to convert in less time than he thought. (*Adjusts shawl over her head.*) Wouldn't that be something, Ron? If I became a Jew in only two or three months?

RON. Fantastic. It took ME nine months.

CHRIS. (*Pours wine into glass with one hand, picks up book with other, reads aloud.*)
Boruch Atoh Adonoy
Elohanu Melech Ha-Olem
Boray Paree Agofen.
Blessed Art Thou, O Lord our God
King of the Universe
Who createth the fruit of the Vine. Amen. (*Drinks.*)

RON. (*Impressed with her dedication.*) Amen. I can't believe this is the same girl I used to know!

CHRIS. (*Lighting candles.*) I'm not. Oh, Ron, I think this is the most meaningful prayer of all. I'll be lighting candles every Friday night and every holiday from now on.

RON. No kidding? I bet even Liberace never lit that many candles.

CHRIS. If a woman like your mother can do it, so can I. (*Candles are lit. SHE picks up the book again, stands and starts to sing:*)

Boruch Atoh Adonoy
Elohanu Melech Ha-Olom
Blessed Art Thou O Lord Our God.

(*And then to RON's astonishment, SHE sets down the book and continues from MEMORY! SHE sings the prayer with absolute solemnity, SHE does all the handwaving motions over the candle bringing the "light" to her face, as though to bring the spirit of the candle into herself.*)

Asher Kid'shanu
B'Mitzvasov V'tzivanu
L'Hadlik Ner Shel Shabbat.
And commanded us to kindle the Sabbath Light
May the Lord Bless us with Sabbath Holiness
May the Lord Bless us with Sabbath Peace. Amen.

(*CHRIS solemnly blows out the candles. NOTE: This is religiously incorrect but she has done this sincerely and respectfully. In other words, she has unwittingly made an error.*)

RON. Oh, honey. I ... I never in a million years would have believed you'd get this involved.

CHRIS. (*Putting everything back into bag.*) I'm so glad you're proud of me, Ron.

RON. ... After all this, I ... I don't know how I'm going to be ... be able to tell you this now.

CHRIS. Tell me what?

RON. Well ... I mean, it's possible—it's just possible it may very well turn out that—that you're doing all this for nothing.

CHRIS. For nothing? What are you talking about?

RON. Well ... even if you do convert ... after you go through with all of this ... I don't see how we can possibly get married now, anyway.

CHRIS. Don't tell me you're converting the *other* way!

RON. Oh, honey, I feel so guilty—after you did all this for me ...

CHRIS. Ron, what are you trying to say?

RON. The reason I got this bursitis attack today—you know how it always comes on when I'm under tension ... my wife called me in the office today.

CHRIS. Your Ex-wife.

RON. My EX-wife. She threatened to take me to court if I don't increase her alimony and child support. She said she can't get along on what I give her.

CHRIS. But you're giving her more than you can afford now.

RON. I called my lawyer. I thought maybe it'd be a good idea to LET her bring me into court. Then I could tell the judge about this middle-aged woman running around with a boy who still goes to college.

CHRIS. That's none of your business. She's not married to you any more. It's *her* life.

RON. Chris, please. I don't need anyone to tell me what is or isn't my business. I pay a lawyer good money for advice.

CHRIS. What did he say?

RON. He said it's not my business any more, it's her life.

CHRIS. So where does that leave US?

RON. Where do you THINK it leaves us? The government says there's no inflation but the way prices keep going up on everything, it's not tough for her lawyer to prove in court that she and the kids can't get along on what I give her. And there's no way I want for my kids to be missing anything they need. I want them to go to the best schools, have the finest clothing, go to camp, whatever makes them happy. So ... I've agreed to give her an increase. I'm sorry, honey, but that means I'll have a lot less to live on myself.

CHRIS. Are you trying to tell me—are you saying that even if I convert, you—you still won't marry me?

RON. Not WON'T marry you, CAN'T marry you. At least not until I'm off the alimony hook for good.

CHRIS. Wait a minute. Let's take this one step at a time, okay? I'm going through with this conversion, no matter what. It's something that's become very important to me. Meanwhile, why don't you have another talk with your ex-wife?

RON. For what? I already had TWO talks with her and neither one did me any good.

CHRIS. When did you have two talks with your ex-wife?

RON. Once when I asked her to marry me and once when she said she wanted a divorce. (*Note: This is a good place to start a very slow, very gradual dimming of the LIGHTS.*)

CHRIS. Ron, we have to know exactly how much more she intends to ask you for. Whatever it is, we'll deal with it. I can get another job or, or who knows, maybe you'll come up with some big money making deal at the office? Anything can happen. Just trust in God.

RON. I DO trust in God! It's my ex-wife's LAWYER who scares the hell out of me!

CHRIS. Will you stop playing around like that with God's name! You have such a religious mother, how come none of it rubbed off on you?

RON. Chris, let's not go through that again, okay? I told you, I'm not against religion.

CHRIS. Never mind what you're not AGAINST! What are you FOR!

RON. Me? I don't know, I ... I guess I'm just for not going through all those old-fashioned rituals with their outmoded customs. In these times, they just don't make any sense any more.

CHRIS. Oh, you're so wrong! It's the rituals that make everything so beautiful! Doing all those things is what makes you PART of it! You have to GIVE something to GET something! The trouble with most people is that when they *need* God, they expect Him to drop everything to help them! You're not the only one He's got on His mind! If you want God when you NEED Him, then WANT Him *before* you need Him!

RON. (*Some of the wind knocked out of his sail.*) Okay, I'm not saying ALL the rituals have no purpose but you gotta admit SOME of them are out of step with the times today.

CHRIS. (*With supreme confidence.*) Which ones? Lighting the candles? Keeping kosher? Setting a table for Passover? Ask me, I know all of them.

RON. Well ... like ... okay, like the rules for not working on the Sabbath. I think—

CHRIS. The Lord has set aside the Sabbath as a Day of Rest and Solemn prayer. You got any objections to that?

RON. (*Losing more confidence.*) No, I think that's a pretty good thing for everyone to follow but—

CHRIS. (*Sardonically.*) Oh, that's so sweet of you, Ron! Oh, God will be so relieved to hear you approve of His ideas!

RON. (*Struggling on.*)—but what was work in the old days when they first wrote the Bible isn't necessarily WORK today. In those days, turning on a light meant going out into the woods and chopping down a tree to start a fire. Okay, THAT was WORK! But today, you're still not allowed to turn on a little light switch! (*Demonstrates by flipping imaginary switch up with index finger crooked.*) What is that, WORK? Try collecting unemployment insurance from laying off doing THIS! (*Repeat same physical biz.*)

CHRIS. But it still has tremendous importance. Maybe not as a FUNCTION but as a TRADITION!

RON. Chris, I believe that if a person feels God within himself, that's good enough.

CHRIS. Well, I don't think it's good enough! That's the lazy man's excuse! The Talmud says "A person BECOMES through his ACTIONS!" People must show their belief in every way possible: THROUGH prayer—THROUGH ritual—THROUGH custom—THROUGH Tradition! Because in those ways, we're showing more than our belief! We're also showing our RESPECT! And Ron, RESPECT is needed in this world today even more than it was in the old days! RESPECT not only for God but for ourselves, our parents, our children and all mankind! I believe there is no other way for the world to survive!

RON. (*Looks at her solemnly, then raises his right hand.*) One Thousand dollars to build the new Hannah Fernandez Temple is contributed by Ron Goldman! ... Anonymously!! (*Embraces her.*) Oh, honey, you're something else.

(*TELEPHONE rings.*)

RON. Was that your phone or mine?
CHRIS. You were talking, I couldn't tell. Shh.

(*THEY listen. It RINGS again.*)

RON. The black one, that's me. (*Goes to phone.*) My poor kids must be worried sick what's keeping me. (*Picks up phone.*) Hello? ... Oh, Alice ... Yes, I was just leaving to pick up the children, tell them I'll be right—Linda's not feeling well? What's wrong with her? (*Listens, then covers mouthpiece, asides to Chris:*) My daughter has a cold. She must have caught it from my ex-wife's boyfriend. You know how kids catch these things from each other. (*Into phone.*) All right, Alice, if you think we should play safe and keep Linda home this week. May I speak to her for a minute? ... Thank you.

CHRIS. If they're not coming, should I unpack?

RON. (*To Chris.*) Only Linda's sick. I'll pick up my son. No way am I going to miss seeing both of them for a whole weekend. (*Into phone.*) Hello, beautiful. This is the man who's going to pick you up in his arms when he sees you and hug you and crush you to pieces in his arms and smother your face with kisses and—what? (*Laughs.*) No! This is not an obscene phone call. (*Still laughing, asides to Chris:*) Did you ever see a sense of humor like that kid's? I swear, that kid should have her own television show! (*Into phone again.*) ... I'll miss you, too, sweetheart. Do you realize this will be the first weekend in five years that you won't be staying with me? ... Honey, when I come by to pick up your brother, how would you like a little present? ... You want me to bring you a what? ... A new ski suit for your Barbi doll? ... I bought you a new ski suit for your Barbie doll last month. What happened to that one? (*Laughing again.*) She OUTGREW IT!!! (*To Chris.*) Don't tell me that kid isn't funnier than Roseanne Barr. (*Into phone.*) Okay, honey, let me speak to your brother. Goodnight, darling, feel better ... I love you too, Princess. Myah! (*That last is a Dinah Shore "smack." Note: By now, it has grown noticeably darker than at beginning of scene.*) Hello, Harvey. Well, it looks like it's you and me alone this weeke— (*Very disappointed.*) You can't see me this week? (*Trying to hide true feelings.*) No, no! Don't feel guilty, son ... Look, I understand. A boy your age has to spend time with his friends, too ... Sure, I can't expect you to spend all your weekends with me now that you're so grown up—(*Indicates to Chris she may as well unpack. SHE takes her bags upstairs.*) ... I'll miss you too, son. ... Then I'll see you next week, okay? (*Disappointed again.*) Ohhh ... Well, how's the weekend after that look to you? ... Okay, Harvey. Listen, I'd appreciate if you let me know when your schedule opens up a little ... I love you, too, son. (*Hangs up, stands a moment, reflecting sadly on changing relationship with his growing son.*) What the hell made me think kids stay kids forever?

(*Now, for the first time, HE becomes aware of how DARK it has become. HE goes to light switch and is about to turn it on when CHRIS comes down.*)

CHRIS. Oh, Ron, now that we're staying home toni— Ron! DON'T!

RON. (*Stops.*) Don't what?

CHRIS. Don't turn on the light!

RON. It's getting dark!

CHRIS. I know. I forgot to turn on the lights before sundown. I thought we'd be leaving.

RON. I've got to turn it on. I want to work on some office papers before dinner.

CHRIS. I can't make dinner now. I didn't turn on the gas in the oven earlier. I'm sorry, Ron, I didn't realize the time before.

RON. In a few minutes, we'll be tripping over each other in the dark!! What are we going to do, Chris?

CHRIS. My name is Hannah.

RON. See that? It's so dark in here, I didn't recognize you! ... Hold it! We can light your candles.

CHRIS. It's too late for that, too! You're not allowed to do any of those things until the Sabbath is over. You can't cook, you can't turn on the lights, you can't carry money, you can't cut pape—Oh, NO!

RON. What's the matter?

CHRIS. I forgot to tear the toilet paper into separate sheets!

RON. THAT I can handle! If it comes to that, I'll use the whole roll in one fell swoop! ... Are you serious? You can't tear *toilet paper*?

CHRIS. The old Talmudic scholars who set these rules decreed that tearing things on the Sabbath is work.

RON. Is there a rule on tearing my hair out? Chris, what are we going to do for the rest of the night? I'm not going to bed at six o'clock just because it's too dark to see in here! (*Glances out patio window.*) Look at that! All the GENTILES are up and having fun!

CHRIS. Ron, I'm sorry. I just need more time to get used to doing these things.

RON. Wait a minute! What am I carrying on? (*Heading for door.*) There's no problem.

CHRIS. Where are you going?

RON. Next door to ask Tommy O'Grady to turn on the lights for us.

CHRIS. It's too late to ASK anyone now. You're supposed to make arrangements like that BEFORE sundown!

RON. They never eat dinner till eight, nine o'clock. To them this is still early.

CHRIS. It doesn't make any difference what time THEY think it is! This is OUR home. *God* will know that we turned the lights on after sundown.

RON. (*Desperately*.) How do you know HE's LOOKING? It's so dark in here, maybe He thinks we went away for the weekend! ... What are we going to do?

(*DOORBELL rings.*)

RON. If that's not a Gentile, please let it be a REFORMED Jew!

(*RON goes to door, opens it. Though it is extremely dark now, from the LIGHT outside, we can see that it is the delivery man.*)

DRIVER. (*Squinting to see in darkness.*) Fernandez? I have some dishes for you.
RON. Come in. Please. Come in.
DRIVER. I have to go back to the truck and get them. Just wanted to make sure someone was home before I carried in a load of three sets of dishes. You opening a restaurant in here? (*Glances in.*) One of them dark, romantic places, huh? (*Starts out.*)
CHRIS. You can save yourself the trouble. I told the store I couldn't accept them if they came after sundown.
DRIVER. Don't worry, ma'am. I have a flashlight.
CHRIS. I'm sorry but you'll have to bring them back Monday. We're not allowed to do business on Friday nights.
DRIVER. You don't have to do any business, ma'am. All you have to do is sign for the delivery.
CHRIS. You don't understand. I can't write.
DRIVER. Oh ... What about your father?
RON. (*Reacts.*) ... Dammit! Even in the DARK???
CHRIS. I'm sorry. He can't write, either.

DRIVER. Funny. I would have sworn you were both college educated people. Okay, be back Monday. (*Starts out.*)

RON. Hold it!

(*The DRIVER pauses.*)

RON. Uhm ... listen, did you—

CHRIS. Ron! You're not allowed to ASK him.

RON. I'm not *asking* anything. (*To Driver.*) I just want to know—did you, uh ... happen to notice there are no lights turned on in here?

DRIVER. (*Peering vainly inside.*) No, I didn't notice. It's too dark in here to see anything.

CHRIS. Ron, I know what you're trying to do but—

RON. I'm not trying to DO anything. I'm merely pointing out to this nice gentleman that we have a problem. I want him to understand that we can't turn on the electric light ourselves because we happen to be religious fanatics.

DRIVER. You got any candles in the house?

RON. Yes but we're not allowed to light candles either. It's already after dark.

DRIVER. It's after dark but you're not allowed to light a candle or turn on the electricity? What is this, some kind of underground religion?

CHRIS. We're religious Jews and it's part of a ritual we have to observe.

RON. (*Hinting broadly.*) But if someone ELSE wanted to turn on the light—purely out of curiosity, you understand—maybe just to SEE what the apartment looks like in the light—we certainly wouldn't be rude enough to STOP them.

(*RON tries to pantomime some indication to the driver that there's a problem with the light. Since he can't come out and ask anything, this gets to be a problem with the DRIVER who is trying hard to guess what Ron seems to be after.*)

DRIVER. (*Finally, gets Ron's message, smiles.*) Where's the switch?

RON. (*Immensely relieved.*) Isn't that funny you should think of that! Right here, sir.

(*CHRIS is appalled as the DRIVER steps inside, turns the light switch on with one index finger.*)

DRIVER. Man! That gives me a feeling of *power*! (*Starts out again.*)

RON. AHMMM!!! ... Before you go—

DRIVER. Yeh?

RON. Would you mind stepping over here a minute?

(*CHRIS knows what he is up to, squirms. The DRIVER looks at Ron in wonderment but follows him to the bathroom.*)

RON. You see ... that's our bathroom—and we're not allowed to TEAR any PAPER, either ... Not ASKING, you understand, just *pointing out*.

DRIVER. Oh!! Yeah, I think I get your problem. (*HE goes into the bathroom.*)

CHRIS. (*Mortified.*) Ron! How could you?

RON. What'd I do? I simply told him what our problem was and he came up with the idea himself. He's a very clever man.

DRIVER'S VOICE. (*From bathroom. His hand sticks a number of torn tissues through the door.*) That enough?

RON. ... Ahm ... We'll be here the whole WEEKEND!

DRIVER'S VOICE. Gotcha. (*Withdraws tissues.*)

CHRIS. (*Livid with rage.*) If I live through this night, I'll see to it that YOU don't!

DRIVER'S VOICE. Think THAT'S enough to hold you?

RON. (*Looks into bathroom.*) Maybe a couple more sheets ... I think we could use a few more short ones, too ... What the hell, let's play safe and go with a half dozen real long ones, just in case—Ah, perfect!

(*CHRIS could strangle Ron. The DRIVER comes out of the bathroom.*)

DRIVER. Well, I'll be back Monday. You want me to bring a paper shredder with me?

RON. No. Thank you. This won't happen again. Now that we can see, we can fix dinn—Whoa! We have an *oven* you might enjoy looking at?

DRIVER. Your oven! Well, if it's anything like the problem with the light switch and the toilet paper, *this* ought to be dynamite! (*Heading for kitchen.*) You're not allowed to turn that on either, huh?

RON. Strictly against the rules.

DRIVER. I gotta look into this religion. You can save a fortune on utility bills alone.

CHRIS. Never mind, thanks. I'm not allowed to *cook* on the Sabbath, either.

DRIVER. Aw, lady, please LET me turn it on. All my other deliveries are so ROUTINE!

CHRIS. That won't be necessary, thank you.

RON. LET him turn the oven on! I don't want to do any cooking! I just want to stick my head in there!

DRIVER. Okay, then. I'll see you people Monday. (*Heads for door.*) And I thought *I* had trouble being BLACK! (*He exits.*)

CHRIS. Ron, if the three rabbis ever find out about this, they'll never accept me.

RON. I'm sorry, honey. I didn't know how else to handle this situation. From now on, we'll have to be more careful when it starts to get dark on Friday evenings. Come on, I'm starved. Let's go into Beverly Hills for dinner.

CHRIS. We're not allowed to *drive*, remember?

RON. Oh, yeah. Okay. there's a nice little restaurant just down the block.

CHRIS. You can't carry money, either.

RON. (*Sure he has her on that one.*) I'll use my credit card.

CHRIS. You can't write. How you going to sign?

RON. Is it a sin to *yell* because I'm getting very nervous!

CHRIS. (*Heading for kitchen.*) I'll open a can of salmon.

RON. You can't use the can opener. It's electric! (*Pantomimes flipping light switch with one finger.*) This is WORK, remember? ... Why couldn't you have converted to something easy like witchcraft? All THEY have to learn is how to shrink heads! ... (*Stymied now, glances at his watch.*) Well ... there's nothing else to do, we may as well go up and watch television.

CHRIS. Electric. (*Pantomimes finger at switch biz.*)

RON. Oh! Yeah ... Well .. there's only one other thing we can do upstairs without turning the light on ... but I'll bet my LIFE that's a NO-NO!

CHRIS. Gee, I'm not sure. The rabbi said it's a blessing for *married* people to have sex on the Sabbath— but he didn't say anything yet about couples who just LIVE together!

RON. (*Heading up stairs as HE unbuttons his shirt.*) Let's try it and see if we're struck by lightning!

(*CHRIS eagerly follow him up the stairs. Suddenly, there is a loud CRACKLING of thunder. LIGHTNING can be seen flashing through the patio door. Terrified, THEY both dash down the stairs to the living room and sit in separate chairs, trying to look as innocent as possible as we bring down LIGHTS fast.*)

ACT II

Scene 1

[If production is using the screen process, flash on picture of crowded southern California beach. Otherwise, while the curtain is still down, we hear the following dialogue on TAPE in the darkness.]
Sound: the OCEAN WAVES under:

WOMAN'S VOICE. Henry, why are you getting up from the beach?

MAN'S VOICE. Just want to see what's going on in the ocean, Margaret.

WOMAN'S VOICE. ... Henry, what are you staring at?

MAN'S VOICE. Nothing, Margaret, just some woman going into the ocean wearing a muu-muu.

WOMAN'S VOICE. Why should a woman go into the ocean wearing a *muu-muu*?

RON'S VOICE. (*Shouting.*) Be careful, Chris! That water's getting a little rough!

STEINBERG'S VOICE. (*Shouting.*) Hannah, take off you muu-muu! Your *muu-muu*! Take it off!

CHRIS'S VOICE. (*Shouting.*) What did you say, Rabbi Steinberg?

STEINBERG'S VOICE. (*Louder.*) I said, "*Take off your muu-muu!*"

RON'S VOICE. (*Louder.*) Chris, be careful! Watch that wave coming at you!

STEINBERG'S VOICE. (*Shouting.*) Hannah! It looks from here like your muu-muu is still touching you! *Remove it so that your body is completely naked*!

WOMAN'S VOICE. (*Quietly.*) ... Henry, where are you going?

MAN'S VOICE. (*Quietly.*) Just going in for a little dip, Margaret.

61

ACT II

Scene 2

In the darkness we hear the sound of an ancient VACUUM CLEANER droning on very loudly in erratic fashion. Nothing else could possibly be heard over this din.

As the LIGHTS come on, the apartment looks particularly spotless. Flowers which weren't there before are now rather conspicuous. Pillows are puffed up. Refreshments have been set out in serving trays. It is obvious that company is expected. RON, in his shirt sleeves, although wearing a tie and grey slacks, is vacuuming the living area rug. His navy blue blazer hangs on the back of a dining chair.

Near the stairs, there is an unoccupied wheel chair. RON moves it aside to clean in that spot, then HE continues on to work in another area as Chris's leg appears at the top of the stairs. It is encased in a plaster of paris cast. SHE is having a very difficult time making her way down the stairs, calling out to Ron who cannot hear her desperate shouts over the noise of the machine. SHE is wearing her best dress and her hair is styled especially attractively today.

As CHRIS descends the steps painfully, SHE yells out to Ron but HE can't hear her. As SHE nears the bottom, SHE reaches out to grab him but misses him as HE goes by.

Finally, SHE gives up the vain effort and struggles over to the wheel chair by herself, and with a herculean effort, SHE just manages to get herself seated, and ends up sitting there, gasping from the exertion.

Now, RON turns off the machine, reels in the electric cord as CHRIS sits in the chair panting. RON calls upstairs:

RON. Honey! I finished vacuuming! I'll be right up to help you down!! (*HE opens the closet door and as HE starts to put machine away, HE becomes aware of Chris's loud gasping and notices her for the first time.*) Why didn't you call me? I would have come up to get you.

CHRIS. (*Gasping from exertion.*) I've been yelling for ten minutes!

RON. I didn't hear you. Was the vacuum making too much noise?

CHRIS. (*Still gasping.*) Noise? At first I thought it was an earthquake! ... Then I was sorry it wasn't.

RON. Take it easy, will you? You're just getting a little edgy because the rabbis will be here any minute.

CHRIS. *You're* looking pretty nervous yourself. What are YOU worried about?

RON. I'm not worried about ANYTHING! I'm Jewish, it's my natural heritage to look worried.... How do you like the way I cleaned the place?

CHRIS. (*Looks around, softens.*) Beautiful, Ron. Hey, you're a regular balabuster.

RON. What's a balabuster?

CHRIS. That's a good housekeeper. How come you don't know what that means?

RON. I don't speak Spanish.

CHRIS. (*Slapping her leg in expression of her annoyance.*) That's JEWISH! Oww! (*The movement has caused a painful reaction to her injured leg.*)

RON. Honey, if your leg hurts that much, maybe you ought to stay in bed.

CHRIS. You crazy? On the most important day of my life?

RON. I'm sure the rabbis will understand. After all, they were there when you had the accident.

CHRIS. They were *there*? *They* CAUSED it! If Rabbi Steinberg hadn't yelled at me from the beach to pull my muu-muu up higher, I would have seen that wave coming. I don't know whether I was more scared or embarrassed out in the middle of the ocean with my leg broken and me without a stitch of clothes on. What took that lifeguard so long to get to me, anyway?

RON. He had to fight off everybody else who wanted to save you.... Chris, are you really sure you want to go through with this?

CHRIS. Give up now? We have a fortune invested in kosher dishes alone! (*Glances at her watch.*) Hey, the rabbis ought to be here any second. Did you hang up the mezzuzzuzum on the door?

RON. The wha—? Yes, I hung up the mezzuzzeh. And I took my name off the door also.

CHRIS. Good. 'Cause the rabbis aren't supposed to know *you* live here, too.

RON. Really? Didn't Steinberg tell them we're living together?

CHRIS. Are you kidding? That's *certainly* not kosher! He said nobody asked him anything, so he never brought it up. The others just took it for granted they're coming over to MY apartment. (*Rubbing her stomach.*) Oh, Ron, I'm getting nervous! My stomach hurts!

RON. You think your stomach hurts *now*? Wait till you start eating Jewish *cooking*!

CHRIS. Ron, my mind! It suddenly went blank! I can't remember any of the lessons I've learned!

RON. Honey, why don't we just postpone this thing until you feel better?

CHRIS. We can't postpone it! This is the only open day the rabbis have on their schedule with the big holidays coming up in two weeks!

RON. Only two more weeks to Christmas?

CHRIS. *Chanukah*!!

RON. (*Chagrined, tries to cover*.) I *meant* Chanukah. Isn't Chanukah the Jewish Christmas?

CHRIS. Chanukah is the Jewish CHANUKAH! I bet you don't even know why this holiday is celebrated. And why we light candles every day for eight days?

RON. ... Uh ... I think I had that one in Trivial Pursuit. Give me a minute ...

CHRIS. (*Following said without stopping*.) "Chanukah is the Feast of Dedication that commemorates our victory of the Maccabeans over the Greek-Syrian King Antiochus, who at one time attempted to utterly destroy the Jewish faith. The Maccabean victory in 165 B.C., was a triumphant vindication of the principle of freedom of religion. Chanukah extends for eight days, from the 25th of Kislev to the 2nd or 3rd of the month of Tebet (depending on whether Kislev has 29 or 30 days). Its distinguishing ceremony is the lighting of the candles each evening, commemorating the rededication of the Temple to the worship of one God by Judas Maccabeus. One candle is lighted on the first evening, two on the second, and so on for each evening of the Festival. At first, it appeared that the oil would last only one evening but miraculously, it lasted for eight days. The lighted menorah, or seven-branched candelabrum became a Jewish symbol of God's word to Zechariah, "Not by might, nor by power, but by My Spirit", says the Lord of Hosts." (*To Ron, triumphantly*.) ... Could YOU learn all that by heart?

RON. I'm still having trouble with *The Star Spangled Banner*.

CHRIS. Oh, Ron, there are so many lovely holidays to celebrate. And I'm going to bring up our children to observe every one of them.

RON. (*A bit edgy now*.) ... What makes you so sure we'll be able to have children?

CHRIS. Why should that be a problem? Every woman in my family makes more babies than Mrs. Fields makes cookies. And *you've* already had two kids yourself, so we're great in that department.

RON. Chris, I ... I didn't want to bring this up before but ... that may have been my entire output.

CHRIS. What are you talking about? I thought your prostate problem was getting better.

RON. Well, it's going bad again. Didn't you hear me pounding the walls and screaming in pain in the bathroom last night?

CHRIS. Was that your prostate? I thought you were yelling like that 'cause I hung up my stockings to dry in there.

RON. Chris, look, I know how much you want children but—

CHRIS. It's not only *children* I want, I want YOU to be their father. Parents like you don't grow on trees ... Okay, maybe monkeys.

RON. Chris, maybe I shouldn't have let you go this far but ... I'm much too old for you. You really need someone closer to your own age.

CHRIS. Ron, cut it out! You know how much time I've wasted trying to talk you out of that dumb idea? If I spent half that time studying to be *Jewish,* I could have been a rabbi by now!

RON. Honey, it's the truth. Maybe it doesn't seem like much difference to you NOW but in a few years—who knows how you'll feel by then? Do you have any idea how fast I'm beginning to age? It's not only my prostate and losing my hair—I'm also shrinking!

CHRIS. NOW YOU'RE SHRINKING? Oh, that's a new one! Oh, *that* tops everything so far! Ron, don't hand me that. You're too young to be shrinking already.

RON. You think so? Well, remember the picture I showed you of me when I was twenty-two years old?? I'm now an inch shorter than that, I checked it.

CHRIS. That's because when you were twenty-two, you had a pompadour this high! (*SHE holds one hand several inches over her head.*)

RON. Thank you very much. You just made me realize I'm now THREE inches shorter.

CHRIS. If *you're* shrinking, so am *I*! So what are you worried? There'll always be the same height difference between us!

RON. I'm a lot older than you! I'm shrinking *faster* than you are! I'll be *passing* you on the way *down!*

CHRIS. You *are* crazy! Maybe *you* ought to convert to *sanity*! Ron, why do you worry about dumb things like that?? No one else but *you* cares about the difference in our ages. The world is changing. This is 1990, we're not in the middle ages.

RON. Maybe *you're* not, *I* am! ... People look at us and they think there's a dirty old man having an affair with a young girl.

CHRIS. It's not an affair, we're going to get married. And please stop calling yourself an old man. You're only forty. I don't consider that old.

RON. No? Well, what's your opinion of forty-two?

CHRIS. Forty-*two*? Ron, what made you think you had to lie to me about two lousy years?

RON. (*Admitting reluctantly.*) Because I didn't have enough nerve to lie about *three* lousy years.

CHRIS. You're forty-*three*??

(*HE nods sheepishly.*)

CHRIS. You idiot! You think age matters to me? What is age? It's only numbers.

RON. I'm glad you feel that way—because I have another number for you. (*Turns away.*)

CHRIS. Forty-*four*? ... Okay, is that it? Is that finally the truth?

RON. That's it. Forty-four.

CHRIS. Not that it matters to me one bit, I'm just curious. Are you forty-four NOW—or are you going to be forty-four on your next birthday?

RON. I'm forty-four NOW ... (*Finding some reason to clean up elsewhere.*) ... on my next birthday I'll be forty-six.

CHRIS. (*Bewildered.*) You mean you're forty-*five*?

RON. Pretty shocked to learn I'm that old, aren't you?

CHRIS. Not really. I'm more shocked to see someone aging so fast right in front of my eyes! ... Then you're forty-five, going on forty-*six*?

RON. (*Nodding.*) That's what I've been trying to tell you, I'm way past my prime.

CHRIS. Aw, baloney. You look just as great *now* as you did a minute ago when you were only forty ...A person is as young as he feels.

RON. Yeah? Well, I feel too old to start my life all over again! Why the hell do I need to get married again at my age? I'm not some hot shot young kid who's got a lifetime of happiness to look forward to! How much time do I have left? I'm forty-seven years old! (*Realizes he has revealed himself.*)

CHRIS. Forty-*seven*? I've had it! I want to see your birth certificate! Right now! Let me see your driver's license!

RON. Forty-seven, I'm forty-seven! Chris, after two marriages, I don't know if I have the energy, the strength to go through that grind all over again.

CHRIS. Ron, let me tell you something. The only reason you're panicking is because the moment of truth is closing in on you. Once those rabbis convert me, we're going to get married. Well, you don't have a thing in the world to worry about. I'm the most perfect girl alive for you. You're insane and only a dummy like me could put up with you.

RON. Chris, I know that y—

CHRIS. Hannah.

RON. Hannah. What happens in a few years when I'm too old to work? How could I support another family? I'm in enough trouble now, working my ass off trying to make enough money to support you and me and an ex-wife and three kids!

CHRIS. THREE kids? You lied about THAT, too! You told me you had only two children.

RON. I'm talking about my wife's boyfriend.

CHRIS. ... Okay, you're getting older, who isn't? All the more reason you should try to find happiness NOW for however many years you have left. ESPECIALLY, if it turns out you're really NINETY years old!

(The DOORBELL rings.)

RON. That must be them!

CHRIS. Omigod, I'm going to pass out!

(RON starts for the door.)

CHRIS. Ron! Put on your coat!

(HE takes coat off from back of chair, puts it on.)

CHRIS. The YAMekee I bought you! Put it on!

(RON takes yarmulke out of pocket.)

CHRIS. Is the kitchen clean?

RON. It's clean! It's spotless!

CHRIS. The fruit! Did you put out the fruit?

RON. It's in the glass bowl. The NEW one. —What am I saying? EVERYTHING's new in here!

CHRIS. Don't say a word about us living together! And try to speak Jewish as much as you can!

RON. I don't KNOW any Jewish!

CHRIS. Oh, Ron! What if I don't pass?

RON. You'll pass! You'll pass! You sound more like my mother than SHE does! (*Hands on doorknob.*) This is your last chance. Want to cross yourself for good luck?

(*CHRIS gestures for him to open it. HE blows her a good luck kiss, opens the door, revealing STEINBERG and two older RABBIS, wearing hats and conservative business suits. Upon entering, each of the two RABBIS will exchange their fedoras for white yarmulkes. THEY also carry velvet bags filled with prayer books and tallethes. [Prayer shawls.]*

STEINBERG. Hello, Mr. Goldman. (*Emphasizing, for other rabbi's benefit.*) I'm glad you could be here at HANNAH'S apartment for this solemn occasion.

RON. Come in, please.

(*ALL THREE enter, each kissing the mezzuzzeh on the door.*)

STEINBERG. You remember Rabbi Rothschild.

RON. (*Nods, shaking rabbi's hand.*) We met at the ocean, at Chri-Hannah's Mikvah.

ROTHSCHILD. (*Is hard of hearing.*) Hah?

RON. (*Louder.*) I said we met at—

ROTHSCHILD. Just a second. (*Reaches into his pocket, takes out a pair of glasses.*) I can't hear a thing without my glasses. That's an old joke but I always get a big laugh with it from everyone. (*Glances at stern-looking Silverman.*) Except him. (*Puts glasses on, now LOOKS directly at Ron's mouth.*)

RON. (*Enunciating carefully.*) We met at the ocean, at Hannah's Mikvah.

STEINBERG. And this is Rabbi Silverman.

SILVERMAN. (*Shaking Ron's hand.*) Hello, again, Mr. Goldman.

RON. Rabbi.

ROTHSCHILD. And how do you feel today, young lady?

CHRIS. (*Her wheel chair not facing him directly.*) Much better, thanks.

ROTHSCHILD. Hah?

CHRIS. (*Spins chair around quickly, to face him.*) Much better, thanks. And I can't tell you how much I appreciate you all coming here.

ROTHSCHILD. Yours is a special case because of your accident. How could we ask you to travel in your condition?

SILVERMAN. Besides, we know how hard you've been working for this. Steinberg here says you are one of the greatest students he's ever had the pleasure of teaching.

STEINBERG. She's just unbelievable the way she's beginning to pick it up.

RON. The Encyclopedia Brittanica calls her whenever they need information on Chanukah.

CHRIS. Won't you gentlemen sit down?

(*SILVERMAN heads for a chair but ROTHSCHILD doesn't hear, continues to stand. SILVERMAN nudges the other man to be seated. ROTHSCHILD sits.*)

CHRIS. Can I offer you some fruit? Some sponge cake? I bought it at a kosher bakery.

SILVERMAN. Do you have kosher dishes?

RON. Does she have kosher dishes? She could cater *three* orthodox weddings simultaneously.

CHRIS. How about you, Rabbi Rothschild?

ROTHSCHILD. If you have kosher dishes, I'll have a glass of tea in a cup.

CHRIS. And you, Rabbi Silverman?

SILVERMAN. Do you have any schnapps?

CHRIS. (*A new word for her.*) Schnapps? ... You mean GINGER schnapps?

RON. He means whiskey. (*To Silverman.*) Yes, we have—SHE has schnapps. (*Heading for the kitchen.*) I happen to know where she keeps it.

CHRIS. (*To Steinberg.*) Anything for you?

STEINBERG. If you have any club soda.

CHRIS. (*Calls out to Ron.*) A glass of club soda for Johnny!

(*ROTHSCHILD and SILVERMAN turn to glare at Steinberg as HE squirms in embarrassment.*)

CHRIS. I thought there were going to be three of you.

SILVERMAN. There are. We'll get started as soon as Rabbi Hahn gets here. He's driving around, trying to find a parking space for his car.

RON. (*From kitchen, as HE works.*) Funny, I always say rabbis should never have trouble finding a parking space. I figure a rabbi could just wave his hands like this— (*Makes "parting of the sea" motion with hands.*)—and all the other cars would part and make room for him.

ROTHSCHILD. (*Laughs.*) That's very funny. (*Then points to the still unsmiling Silverman.*) That's the biggest laugh anyone ever got from him.

SILVERMAN. I take it you're not a very religious man, Mr. Goldman.

RON. Me? Oh ... uh ... I guess you could say I was sort of ... average religious.

SILVERMAN. Does that mean you're one of those part-time worshippers who go to Synagogue only once a year on the holidays?

RON. Ohh ... not ... THAT often ...

SILVERMAN. When *was* the last time you went to Shul?

RON. (*Feeling uncomfortable.*) ... Shul: You mean Synagogue? The last time I went to Shul? ... I guess ... when ... my son was Bar Mitzvahed last year.

SILVERMAN. And before then?

RON. (*Admits grudgingly.*) ... When *I* was Bar Mitzvahed.

ROTHSCHILD. You didn't go to Shul in all the years in between?

RON. (*Squirming.*) ... Well ... sure I did.

ROTHSCHILD. How often did you go?

RON. Uh ... just *once* ... when my father died.

ROTHSCHILD. ... Is that what killed him?

CHRIS. (*Trying to get Ron off the hook.*) ... His *mother* is a very religious woman.

SILVERMAN. (*Icily.*) Really? What religion is that?

ROTHSCHILD. Mr. Goldman, would you mind telling me? Did you ever lay Tvillin?

CHRIS. Tvillin who?

STEINBERG. (*After a long, embarrassing moment, jumps in trying to save the day.*) ... Tvillin! The leather straps we bind around our arms when we offer the daily prayers! It's called "Laying Tvillin."

RON. (*Coming out of kitchen with tray.*) Hokay! Rabbi Silverman gets the schnapps—(*To Steinberg.*)—and yours is the club soda.

ROTHSCHILD. What about the hot water?

RON. I'm getting deeper into tha—oh, you mean for the tea! That's coming along. (*Retreats hastily toward kitchen.*)

CHRIS. (*Anxious to change subject, Looks out window.*) Ron! I think I see a parking space opening up across the street. Why don't you go out and see if you can hold it for Rabbi Hahn?

RON. (*Gratefully heads for door.*) Right. That's a great idea.

STEINBERG. (*Also heads for door.*) You hold the space, I'll try to find the rabbi.

(*STEINBERG gets to door before Ron, opens the door and kisses the mezzuzzeh. RON follows him but forgets to kiss it. ROTHSCHILD hasn't seen, is wiping his glasses.*)

SILVERMAN. Mr. Goldman!
RON. (*Stops, worried.*) Yes?
SILVERMAN. You just went out the door.
RON. (*Confused.*) I know.
SILVERMAN. Did you forget to kiss something?

(*RON is lost for a moment, then assumes Rabbi could only mean Chris, heads back toward her, passing Silverman.*)

SILVERMAN. Not HER!

(*Again, RON stops. If not Chris, then who? HE guesses, shrugs and goes to Silverman, puckering his lips. Just before HE reaches Silverman's cheek, STEINBERG calls out:)*

STEINBERG. The MEZZUZZEH!!

(RON stops, is pretty shaken up, heads out, kissing the mezzuzzeh on the way, STEINBERG following.)

SILVERMAN. Well, Rothschild, what did you think of that?

ROTHSCHILD. What happened? I didn't hear a word, I was cleaning my glasses.

SILVERMAN. *(Dismisses him.)* Hannah, as soon as Rabbi Hahn gets here, we shall ask you certain questions to determine whether or not—

(BOAT WHISTLE.)

ROTHSCHILD. Hah! My tea is ready!

CHRIS. No, that's a boat.

SILVERMAN. Hannah, my dear, this is one of the greatest days of your life.

CHRIS. Yes, I know.

SILVERMAN. It is a day in which you will be tested to see how much you have learned about our religious laws and customs and history and traditions, which will determine whether or not you are prepared to take your place in the world as a Jew. It is a day to be marked down in your Book of Life as one which will change the course of everything you do and think from this day forward. It is a day in which—

ROTHSCHILD. Silverman, if you don't cut it short, the day will be over already.

SILVERMAN. I have to ask her if she's aware of the magnitude of the step she is about to take, don't I?

ROTHSCHILD. Steinberg says there aren't too many around like her. I don't want to lose this one before we begin.

SILVERMAN. What kind of talk is that, Rothschild? You know we never do any recruiting for converts.

ROTHSCHILD. Who's recruiting? I just don't want to see this one discharged before she enlists.

SILVERMAN. Hannah, we never proselytize. You must understand it is our solemn duty to make absolutely certain this is something YOU want with all your heart. That's why we always try to make converting as difficult as possible for everyone.

CHRIS. There were a couple of times I thought I'd never make it. But Rabbi Steinberg helped me through. He has the patience of a *saint*.

(*ROTHSCHILD and SILVERMAN turn to look at each other*.)

ROTHSCHILD. Hannah, my child, you have had ample time to see what the life of an orthodox Jew will be like.

SILVERMAN. You know now all that is expected of you. Are you absolutely certain you can keep it up for the rest of your life?

ROTHSCHILD. Hannah, are you willing to forsake your past religion?

SILVERMAN. Do you want to change your mind? If your answer is no, we will start the moment Rabbi Hahn gets here.

(*TELEPHONE rings*.)

ROTHSCHILD. (*With confidence*.) THAT'S a boat!
SILVERMAN. *That's* a telephone!

(ROTHSCHILD shrugs in defeat. CHRIS hasn't moved. The OTHERS look at her expectantly. The PHONE rings again.)

SILVERMAN. Hannah ... the phone is ringing. Would like me to get it for you?
CHRIS. Is it—is it the black one or the white one?

(PHONE rings again.)

SILVERMAN. The white one.
CHRIS. *(Relieved.)* OH, good, I'll take it.

(SILVERMAN picks up the white phone and hands it to her.)

CHRIS. Hello—

(The black PHONE rings again as CHRIS reacts in dismay as SHE holds the dead line.)

SILVERMAN. *(Shrugs.)* I was wrong, it was the black one. *(Picks it up before Chris can stop him.)* Hello, Miss Fernandez's apartment ... Yes, of course, this is her phone ... Who is this? *(Covers mouthpiece.)* It's a little boy, says he's Mr. Goldman's son.
CHRIS. *(Flusters.)* Oh! Uh ... yes ... Ron probably told him he'd be visiting here today.
SILVERMAN. *(Nods, speaks into phone.)* Would you like to hold, your father will be right back.... What do you mean, "why did I say this is Miss Fernandez's apartment"? ... Because it IS her apart—You're wrong, sonny. How could this be your *father's* apartment when SHE lives here— *(Beginning to get the idea.)*—you call your father ALL the time and THIS is where he lives? ... I see ... Ahh,

young man, why don't I have your father call you when he gets back? ... Very good. Goodbye. (*Is about to hang up, puts phone to mouth again.*) Uh, just a minute. I was wrong. Yes, this IS your father's apartment. (*HE hangs up.*)

(*CHRIS can't find the right words to explain this unexpected turn.*)

SILVERMAN. (*Indignantly.*) You invite us to your home where you live in SIN?—Rothschild! Don't drink from that cup! It's Trayf!

ROTHSCHILD. (*The cup of tea poised to his lips. Puts it down.*) What a close call! My whole life started to flash before me!

(*The TWO RABBIS start for the door, taking off their yarmulkes and replacing them with their hats.*)

CHRIS. I didn't mean to do anything wrong. I admit THAT's why I wanted to convert at first, just to get married but—

(*Stops as SHE realizes this admission is only making things worse. The TWO RABBIS continue toward the door as it opens and RON and STEINBERG enter.*)

RON. We can't find Rabbi Hahn. He must be driving around the other side of the marin—Hannah! What happened?

CHRIS. (*Somberly.*) You can call me Chris again.

RON. I don't understand.

SILVERMAN. Your son just called.

CHRIS. On the BLACK telephone. Rabbi Silverman picked it up and told him it was MY apartment.

RON. Oh no! Then the boy KNOWS!

SILVERMAN. (*Nods.*) I'm sorry. I felt so terrible when I realized—I told him you would call him back.

(*RON goes to phone quickly, dials.*)

SILVERMAN. (*Starts for door.*) Well, there's no need for Rabbi Hahn to find a parking space now. Come, Rothschild, let's wait for him outside.

CHRIS. Please! Wait!

(*Near the door, the RABBIS hesitate.*)

CHRIS. I don't know how to make you believe this—okay, I admit that's the way it started. Yes, at first I wanted to become Jewish just to get married but ...

RON. Alice! Let me speak to Harvey.

CHRIS. (*In tears.*) ... but since I started studying ... it ... it's become the most important thing that's ever happened to me—

RON. Harvey! Please listen to me!

CHRIS. I've done all the things I'm supposed to do. Ask me the questions, you'll see how much I know about keeping kosher and all the holiday prayers—

RON. It's not like you think, son.

CHRIS. Rabbi Steinberg, please tell them how hard I worked. Remember at the beginning, you thought I couldn't do it? Remember how bad I was that time when Ron came home and you met him that day?

SILVERMAN. (*To Steinberg, shocked.*) You KNEW they were living together in sin all this time?

STEINBERG. I ... I could see how much she loved him. And they WERE going to get married...

RON. Harvey, I didn't want you to know because I was afraid you wouldn't understand ...

SILVERMAN. THIS is the kind of rabbi we were considering to take over our congregation some day? To lead our young and set an example for them?

ROTHSCHILD. What did you have in mind for the boys you were preparing for Bar Mitzvah? To give them fountain pens filled with marijuana?

RON. Son, all I want is a chance to explain.

STEINBERG. I just didn't feel I had the right to judge another human being.

SILVERMAN. You don't. And you have even less right to teach anyone. I'll take over the Bar Mitzvah class myself until you can be replaced.

(*BOAT WHISTLE.*)

ROTHSCHILD. Hannah, your other phone is ringing.

SILVERMAN. That's a *boat*!

ROTHSCHILD. (*Shrugs helplessly.*) There's no use, I gotta get new glasses.

RON. Just know one thing, Harvey. Everything I've ever done in my life, I did only for my children.... I love you, son. (*Hangs up.*)

CHRIS. Will it be all right?

RON. He's pretty shook up. Not so much because he knows now we live together—he says he can handle that. What bothers him is that I lied to him. That's the only time in my life I've ever lied to him. More than anything else, I've taught my children never, never to lie. Wow! You spend a child's whole lifetime trying to teach them respect and a sense of values—and with one phone call, it's all wiped out.

(*The DOORBELL rings.*)

ROTHSCHILD. I'd go crazy living here with those boat whistles all day long.
CHRIS. That's the *doorbell.*
ROTHSCHILD. (*To Chris.*) Do you have any aspirins?
CHRIS. Yes but I'm not sure if they're kosher.

(*The DOORBELL rings again.*)

STEINBERG. That must be Rabbi Hahn.

(*HE opens the door to admit a smartly dressed WOMAN in her early seventies but extremely vital and energetic.*)

WOMAN. Boy, it's murder trying to find a parking space around here—what's going on, a party?
RON. (*Stunned.*) What are YOU doing here?
WOMAN. I stopped off on my way to the airport. I'm going to Vegas for the weekend with my boyfriend.
RON. (*Still surprised by visitor.*) ... Hannah ... Rabbis ... this is my mother.

(*EVERYONE is stunned.*)

CHRIS. THAT'S the lady you told me that whole story about???!!!
WOMAN. Oh, thank you. (*Going to Chris with a smile.*) And what's this adorable little thing doing here?
SILVERMAN. (*With self-righteous indignation.*) She LIVES here!
WOMAN. (*To Ron.*) Don't tell me you've adopted another child!!

(*And as RON reacts at that latest slap to his ego and pride, we ... go to BLACK.*)

ACT II

Scene 3

*It is several minutes later. MRS. GOLDMAN is the only
one onstage. SHE is talking on the telephone, standing
near the vacant wheel chair DS ... fingering it absently.*

MRS. GOLDMAN. ... Arthur, I'll tell you everything
that went on here on the plane to Las Vegas. ... Arthur, I
don't *want* to tell you NOW. ...because I'm afraid you
might change your mind about me when you hear what a
yutz I have for a son. (*Out of curiosity, sits in wheelchair.*)
... No, I'll be here at least another hour or so.... Arthur, I
can't leave my boy when he's feeling down like this. I've
never seen him so broken up about losing a woman before
... What? ... Why does every woman he falls in love with,
finally dump him? Because he only falls in love with
intelligent women, that's why. ... Arthur, I can't talk any
more, someone's coming. I'll meet you at the airport in
an hour.

(*SHE hangs up as RON now comes down the stairs
carrying Chris's suitcases.*)

MRS. GOLDMAN. Well, how'd it go up there?
RON. (*Setting bags down near door.*) It's all over
between us.
MRS. GOLDMAN. You and Chris are really finished?
RON. And Hannah, too. The three of us are splitting
up.
MRS. GOLDMAN. I don't blame her. How could you
have lied to her like that?—Telling her I was an old lady!

Ugghhh!!! (*Groans from creaky bones as SHE gets out of chair with some difficulty.*)

RON. I couldn't think straight at the time. I kept trying to think up all kinds of reasons to avoid getting married. She had an answer for every one—so, finally, out of desperation, it just popped into my head to tell her you were very religious.

MRS. GOLDMAN. (*Putting phone back in place.*) I don't understand you. How could you even *think* of something like that?

RON. I don't know, I—I thought I once heard you say you light candles on Friday nights.

MRS. GOLDMAN. I light candles EVERY night. They hide wrinkles better than electric lights.

RON. Mom, do you really think I would have come up with an idea like that if I thought she would actually convert?

MRS. GOLDMAN. When you saw her begin to take lessons in Judaism, why didn't tell her the truth *then*?

RON. By that time, she'd become the most religious person I ever saw! Every day she was getting closer and closer to God. I was afraid if she got mad at me, she could create a FAMINE and a PESTILENCE in here! ... Anyway, what do you think of her?

MRS. GOLDMAN. From everything you told me, she seems to be a wonderful young woman.

RON. I didn't even tell you half. She's incredible.

MRS. GOLDMAN. Then all I have to say is when you've lived as long as I have, you learn to take a little happiness whenever you're lucky enough to find it.

RON. Mom, are you saying—do you mean it wouldn't bother you if I married a twenty-six year old girl?

MRS. GOLDMAN. Better than my friend Minnie. Her son married a twenty-six year old BOY!

RON. I can't believe it! I thought for sure you'd hit the ceiling if you knew I was involved with someone so much younger than me.

MRS. GOLDMAN. Ronnie, sweetheart, there's only one thing that matters. You both love each other. It's no one else's business that she's twenty-six and you're past fifty.

RON. *SH!!!* Mom, will you keep quiet! (*Rushes to foot of stairs, looking up, worried that Chris might have heard.*) She thinks I'm only forty-sev—Agh, what the hell difference does it make now?

MRS. GOLDMAN. Dum dum, you finally have a chance for a little happiness, why don't you grab it?

RON. And how long do you think that happiness can last? In ten years, I'll be sixty and she'll be thirty-six and it'll be all over between us.

MRS. GOLDMAN. That's right. You'll be out looking for twenty-six year olds again ... Oh, Ronnie, baby, you're your father all over again. He lived in constant fear of all the awful things he THOUGHT were going to happen in his life but nothing that terrible ever came about. Give yourself a chance, maybe something wonderful could happen to you. Who knows? Sometimes God takes pity on people. Didn't he finally stop the country from making Dan Quayle vice-president jokes?

RON. Mom, I'm a two time loser. I've suffered enough PAIN in my life. The thought of possibly making another mistake scares the hell out of me.

MRS. GOLDMAN. What are you looking for, guarantees in life? There are none! That's why *I* live for TODAY.

RON. Oh, really? Is that why you're carrying on like you are? Aren't you ashamed of yourself running off with some guy for a weekend in some cheap, sleazy hotel in Las Vegas?

MRS. GOLDMAN. How dare you accuse me of a thing like that? Arthur's paying over three hundred dollars a day for our room! ... Oh, stop looking so worried, we're going there to get married.

RON. *Married*? When you walked in here, why did you let me think you were on your way to have an *affair* with some guy? Why didn't you just say you were getting MARRIED?

MRS. GOLDMAN. Because knowing how *you* feel about getting married, I was afraid you'd be ashamed of me! ... I have to admit I was pretty surprised to learn you were living with someone. How long has *that* been going on?

RON. About a year. We kept it quiet because I didn't want my kids to know what was going on.

MRS. GOLDMAN. How did you manage to keep them from finding out?

RON. That was the easy part. Whenever any of them called me, it was on the black phone. When anyone called Chris, it was on the white phone. Does that shock you?

MRS. GOLDMAN. Not a bit. Whenever *you* called *me*, it was on my RED phone. When Arthur's family called, it was on his BLUE phone! ... Does that shock YOU?

RON. Me? Of course not, why should—YES, if you want to know the truth, it shocks the hell out of me!

MRS. GOLDMAN. Oh, really? Tell me why is it all right for *you* but not for *me?*

RON. You're my MOTHER!

MRS. GOLDMAN. You're my SON!

RON. (*Bewildered.*) That makes absolutely no sense at all!

MRS. GOLDMAN. That's what I told the obstetrician when he delivered you but he insisted *you* were my child all right!

RON. Weren't you afraid someone in our family might find out you're living with this man?

MRS. GOLDMAN. How? Who ever comes to visit? ... And I wouldn't have kept it a secret if I wasn't so worried how *you* would react to it. You're a hundred years behind the times and that's the way you were from the day you were born. That would have made some story in today's tabloid papers: "Woman gives birth to child older than she is!"

RON. Mom, this is your fourth marriage. If things were going so well for you living together, why do you have to get married again at your age?

MRS. GOLDMAN. (*Proudly.*) For two good reasons: One, I don't like being lonely any more than you do. And two, *I* believe in marriage. Every one of my marriages was a fabulous success. Not one ended in divorce. They all *died*!

RON. Well, you're lucky. Both times I was married, I thought my ex-wives and I were really in love. But each one ended in disaster. How can I be sure it won't happen again?

MRS. GOLDMAN. Don't marry your ex-wives again ... Ronnie, sweetheart, just because you've been hurt twice before, doesn't mean it will happen again. When people fall off a horse, they pick themselves up and try again. Don't you think that's what YOU should do?

RON. Yes. If I ever decide to marry a horse, that's what I'll do.

MRS. GOLDMAN. Ronnie, baby, you've got to stop clutching on to all those bad memories and move ahead with your life! Don't you see what you're doing, darling? You couldn't make either of your marriages work, so you're trying to hold your divorces together.

RON. That's the most ridiculous thing I ever heard!

MRS. GOLDMAN. Wrong. The most ridiculous thing you ever heard is every time you open your mouth. Why don't you try opening your EYES and take a good look at yourself? Maybe you'll see the *real* reason you're afraid to marry this girl.

RON. Mom, there's only one reason: I lived through enough pain. My first divorce was bad enough without children but the second time, when my kids were involved—I mean, suddenly having them taken away from me and uprooting me from my home. How could my wife do that to me?

MRS. GOLDMAN. That's EX-wife! When are you going to let go? You know something, your divorces are in worse trouble than your marriages were ... The truth, my dear son, is NOT that you're afraid to suffer any more PAIN. What you're really afraid of is being HAPPY!

RON. Mom, whenever I hear you say things like that, I get the feeling when I was a child, someone abandoned me on the door of some mental institution and you were the kook who came out to pick me up!

MRS. GOLDMAN. If I'm crazy, I inherited it from you! (*SHE reacts to her own comment, realizing it made no sense.*)

RON. Mom, let's drop this whole discussion, okay? Go, go on your honeymoon, your groom is waiting.

MRS. GOLDMAN. My honeymoon can wait. At Arthur's age, how much can happen when we get there, anyway? ... And since you asked, I'll tell you something else about yourself.

RON. When did I ASK anything? Who heard me ask anything?

MRS. GOLDMAN. Not only does the thought of being *happy* scare the pants off you—what you *really* want to do is LIVE IN PAIN! ... Oboy, would that make you happy!

RON. It would make me happy to *live in pain*??

MRS. GOLDMAN. You would rather live in pain than on the Riviera!

RON. What are you talking ab—? I hate pain! I love being happy! I'm happy lots of times. I'm not saying I'm happy every minute but whenever I'm happy, there's no one I enjoy being with more than me ... If I was an unhappy man, would I be going through life making jokes all the time? Don't I always make everyone laugh?

MRS. GOLDMAN. Yes. But never when you're trying to say something funny!

RON. Mom, it's wonderful having these heart to heart talks with you every fifty years or so but—

MRS. GOLDMAN. Will you listen and try to learn something? The reason you enjoy living in pain is because it's something you're *familiar* with. And because you're familiar with it, you're *comfortable* with it! That's why you're afraid to marry this girl—even though she might make you happy beyond your wildest dreams—because that would mean having to make A CHANGE IN YOUR LIFE! But you're afraid of CHANGE—simply because the happier life you might possibly CHANGE to is *unfamiliar* to you!

RON. (*Genuinely impressed.*) I never heard you talk this way before. How did you learn all this modern psychology?

MRS. GOLDMAN. Because I'm not like you. I'm not afraid of change. I want to improve the quality of my life every way I can. That's why I enrolled in an adult education course at UCLA. That's where I met Arthur.

RON. Oh. Does he teach the class?

MRS. GOLDMAN. No, he works in the cafeteria.

(*RON throws up his hands helplessly.*)

MRS. GOLDMAN. And now I'll tell you something I didn't have to go to school to learn: You're the world's most loving father. That's wonderful. But since your divorce, you've been sacrificing your *own* life for the sake of your children. And that's not wonderful. Ronnie, YOU have to be happy, too. If YOU'RE happy, the children will be happy. And if you don't think of your own future happiness now— one day, and this may be hard for you to believe—when those kids grow up, they may not have as much time for YOU as they do now. They'll want to be with their own friends—

(RON looks thoughtful, recalling similar experience with his son.)

MRS. GOLDMAN. —and later with their own husbands and wives and after that, with their own children. That doesn't mean they don't love you, darling, that's the way of life. Ronnie, baby, I'm not saying anything any NORMAL person doesn't know, I'm just saying it to YOU.

RON. Mom, I love you. I try to see you as much as I can, it's just so hard to find time for everything—

MRS. GOLDMAN. I know that, darling. And just because I'm bawling the crap out of you now doesn't mean I don't love you. You'll learn some day when you get to be my age that—

RON. Mom, YOU never got to be your age.

MRS. GOLDMAN. When you get older, if you don't have someone to share your life with, will you be able to face a life alone like you'll have to if that girl leaves you like the others did? So, what do you say, darling, are you going to take a chance and marry this girl or not?

RON. What is this with you pushing so hard for me to *marry* her? What are you, MY mother or HER mother?

MRS. GOLDMAN. Sweetheart, you've got to wake up and change. Come on, baby, chase out all that ugly pain that's been eating you up and start enjoying life! From now on, live to be happy! Come on, darling, say it together with me: "Goodbye Pain! Hello Happiness!" Let me hear it: "Goodbye Pain. Hello Happiness!"

(Unseen by either RON or his mother, CHRIS has been laboriously coming down the stairs.)

CHRIS. "Hello Happiness, Goodbye Ron." *(Hobbling over to wheel chair.)* You can live with the *pain* without getting married, but not with *me*. Will you please call me a taxi?

RON. *(Turns, sees her.)* Chris! ... Why can't we go on the way it was?

CHRIS. Because nothing IS the way it WAS any more. You're such a liar, that even when it WAS that way, that's not the way it was 'cause it never was the way you said it was—I don't know what I'm saying, I just want to get out of here.

RON. Chris, I never meant to hurt you. I'm sorry I exaggerated about my mother being so religious—

CHRIS. EXAGGERATED? You didn't exaggerate, you lied! I bet you even lied about being forty-seven! I bet you're forty-*eight*!

RON. You caught me again.

MRS. GOLDMAN. *(Reacts to that lie.)* I don't want to be your mother any more, you hear me? From now on, we're COUSINS! ... DISTANT cousins! And I'll get my lawyer to make that *legal!*

RON. Mom, I'm trying! When you've been lying as much as I have, it's hard to quit cold turkey!

CHRIS. *(Wheeling chair to phone.)* I'll call a cab myself.

RON. Chris, wait! Please. *(To Mother.)* Mom ... there's something I want to say to Chris right now and ...

I'm sorry but it's a little difficult to talk with someone else around ...

MRS. GOLDMAN. Oh! I'm sorry! Go ahead, sweetheart, I'll use the guest bathroom. I want to freshen my perfume, anyway. (*Taking bottle of perfume out of bag as SHE heads for bathroom.*) It's Arthur's favorite. I use it to revive him all the time. (*SHE goes into bathroom.*)

RON. Chris, I just had a long talk with my mother and she made me see things that I never—

MRS. GOLDMAN. (*Calls out, from inside bathroom.*) What kind of lunatic guests do you have? Did you know someone tore up all your toilet paper?

RON. (*Reacts in annoyance, then goes on.*) Chris ... okay, maybe it's time for me to admit to myself the truth about why I'm so desperately afraid to get married—despite the fact that I'm crazy in love with you.

CHRIS. Ron, see how hard this cast is? (*SHE raps on it with knuckle.*) If this is another lie, I'm going to kick you in a place that will make you talk in such a high voice no one will understand you, anyway.

RON. The truth, I swear ... Chris, you were never divorced. You don't know how guilty I felt because of my children. Well, I believe kids shouldn't have to suffer because of their parents mistakes. So after my divorce, I tried to compensate—okay, maybe over-compensate—for them not having a father around during their growing up years. That's why, whenever I met a woman who was getting too close to me, somehow, I ... I found a way to kill that relationship because I was afraid it would cut down on the time I'm able to spend with my children *now*. Don't you see, I want to give my kids the opportunity to be with ME, to see ME for as much time as I can possibly be with them.

MRS. GOLDMAN. (*From inside bathroom.*) That's the worst case of child abuse I ever heard!

RON. Mom, please! ...

CHRIS. Ron, don't you think I've known that all this time?

RON. (*Surprised.*) You did?

CHRIS. Of course. My parents were divorced, too. That's why I went through all the inconvenience I did to allow you to see your children as much as you wanted to. And because I knew what you were going through, it only made me love you more. Ron, let me into that part of your life and share your love for your children with you.

RON. Oh, sweetheart! (*Embraces her.*) Does that mean you'll change your mind about leaving?

CHRIS. (*Thinks for a short moment.*) ... Yeah, okay, I'll stay! On one condition: if in the next ten seconds, I hear a proposal of marriage! Okay, you've got ten seconds. Start your heart attack now!

(*SHE counts and keeps looking at her watch as RON is torn but can't come to a decision.*)

CHRIS. ... seven ... eight ... nine ... I'm leaving if I don't hear a proposal—

MRS. GOLDMAN. (*From inside bathroom.*) ALL RIGHT! CHRIS, WILL YOU MARRY MY SON?!

(*CHRIS reaches for the phone.*)

RON. Chris, I swear to you—there's nothing more I want than to marry you—but I ... I just can't.

CHRIS. Why not? Don't tell me you lied about your age again? (*Guessing.*) You're under twenty-one!

RON. No, I'm perfectly free to get married—

CHRIS. Then there's only one other thing. You're still in love with your—

RON. No, I'm not still in love with my wife.

MRS. GOLDMAN. (*Coming out of bathroom.*) I told you! That's EX-wife! Like when a relationship's over, it's over. Like in EX-mother!

CHRIS. I don't get it. You love me, you WANT to marry me. You're free but you *won't* marry me! What is it, Ron? Is it because some day I'm going to be taller than you? I give up, Ron. You're too much for me.

RON. Wrong, Chris. I'm not enough for you. Don't you see? *Knowing* what my problem is doesn't mean I can change overnight. I ... I need more time to adjust to this new way of thinking.

CHRIS. But you're willing to take a chance on losing me? You said you're afraid you're getting shorter? You're not getting shorter, Ron. You just LOOK shorter 'cause your head is missing! Out of my way!

(*SHE starts for the door as the DOORBELL rings. RON opens it. It is STEINBERG.*)

STEINBERG. I'm sorry to bother you.

RON. (*Shrugs disconsolately.*) The last time a rabbi bothered me was with a little knife forty years ago— (*Glances toward Chris, confesses.*) forty-*seven* years ago.

CHRIS. (*Triumphantly.*) Forty-*eight* years ago!

MRS. GOLDMAN. FIFTY years ago!

(*That comes as a surprise to Chris. MRS. GOLDMAN grins smugly at her little revelation. RON acknowledges defeat with a nod.*)

RON. Would you like to come in?

(*STEINBERG kisses the mezzuzzeh and enters. HE is followed by RABBI HAHN, who also kisses the mezzuzzeh.*)

STEINBERG. This is Rabbi Hahn. Rabbi, you remember Mr. Goldman from the ocean. And this is MRS. Goldman.

HAHN. (*Is serious, no flattery here.*) MRS. Goldman? You told me he was divorced.

(*MRS. GOLDMAN grins broadly, simply adoring that mistaken "association" with her son but RON isn't too happy.*)

MRS. GOLDMAN. I'm his kid mother.

STEINBERG. And of course, you remember Hannah from the Mikvah. The young lady who wants to convert.

CHRIS. Who WANTED to convert. I guess that's all over now, huh?

HAHN. Not necessarily.

CHRIS. You mean there's still a chance for me?

HAHN. Well ... yes and no.

RON. You're going to let her become HALF Jewish?

HAHN. I just heard one version from my colleagues outside and I heard another version from— (*Glares at Steinberg.*)—the basketball coach here. Now I'd like to hear *your* story, young lady.

(*CHRIS doesn't know where to start.*)

STEINBERG. You can speak freely. The rabbi knows all about you wanting to convert only to get married.

CHRIS. Well, that may have been true once but not any more.

STEINBERG. See! That's what I told you, Rabbi.

HAHN. You also told me our team would be undefeated this year! We won one game out of fifteen. And *that* on a forfeit because the other team didn't show up. THEY remembered it was a Sabbath but *he* didn't.

STEINBERG. (*Embarrassed, to Chris.*) I was confused that day. I had my mind filled with ways to resolve our— *your* situation.

HAHN. So, I have an important decision to make here. First, I would like to know, do you *still* want to become Jewish?

CHRIS. Oh, yes. Is it still possible.

HAHN. Well ... yes and no.

RON. Rabbi, can't you decide one way or the other? She just wants to know, does she fast on Yom Kippur or go shopping on Christmas?

HAHN. This is not a decision to be taken lightly. Please don't rush me, young man.

RON. (*Grandiosely appreciative.*) Anybody that calls me "young man" can take as much time as he likes.

HAHN. As I see things, it isn't up to us to make God's decisions for Him. It is up to us only to *interpret* His laws. I don't feel we have the right to judge others.

STEINBERG. That's exactly what *I* said!

HAHN. (*Annoyed with younger man.*) If that's what YOU said, I may change my mind. (*To others.*) The question then is, what is sin? Is it a sin for a man and a woman to live together without being married?

MRS. GOLDMAN. (*Pushing others aside to get closer.*) Excuse me, this *I* want to hear!

HAHN. And if it IS a sin, is the sin forgiven if the couple gets married?

CHRIS. But, Rabbi, we're not getting married.

HAHN. You're not getting married? (*To Steinberg.*) You didn't tell me that.

STEINBERG. SHE didn't tell ME that, either.

CHRIS. (*Indicating Ron.*) That's 'cause HE just told me that.

HAHN. In that case, I can make a decision. ... Since the couple in question is NOT getting married, at least ONE question will have been answered: We know now, for certain, that the girl wants to become Jewish for that reason and that reason ALONE—and not merely because she wishes to get married.

CHRIS. Then I *can* become Jewish?

HAHN. ... Well ... yes and no.

(The OTHERS react in ad-lib VOCAL frustration.)

HAHN. Since the girl in question is not going to marry the man in question, I would say it is STILL possible for her to go through with the conversion — if ... the girl stops living with the man.

CHRIS. *(Indicating her bags near door.)* That's marvelous. I was just moving out, anyway.

STEINBERG. You're really leaving him?

CHRIS. I'm moving in with my girl friend, Doris.

HAHN. Then there's no longer any problem.

CHRIS. Well, maybe there is? Is it all right for me to live with her? She happens to be a shiska.

HAHN. A shiska? — Oh, you mean a Gentile girl!

CHRIS. *(To Ron, triumphantly.)* See? EVERYONE knows the word except you!

HAHN. Well, since that's all settled, there is no longer any problem. After you've gotten yourself settled in your new apartment, get in touch with me after Chanukah and I'll schedule another meeting. As for you, Steinberg, because of your youth and inexperience and because in your heart you meant well, I have decided to give you another chance.

STEINBERG. Thank you, Rabbi Hahn. You won't regret keeping me on.

HAHN. I'm not so sure. I still have to break that depressing news to our poor basketball team.

CHRIS. I'm sorry you had so much trouble finding a parking space, Rabbi.

HAHN. Me? I was just lost. Finding a space is never a problem for me.

(*HE turns to head out, only to find the door blocked by all the OTHERS. HE makes a "parting of the sea" motion with his hands, and miraculously, THEY all part to make a path for him. He EXITS, kissing the mezzuzzeh on the way.*)

CHRIS. Jonas, could you please give me a lift to my girl friend's place in Santa Monica?

STEINBERG. My pleasure. (*HE picks her up in his arms.*)

RON. Chris, please don't walk out on me again.

CHRIS. (*Haughtily.*) I'm not walking out ... I'm being CARRIED out! (*Gestures for Steinberg to continue.*)

RON. Chris! Please, I don't know what I'd do without you.

CHRIS. Oh, Ron, there's plenty for you to do. You can start by pasting together a whole roll of toilet paper.

(*SHE nods to Steinberg and HE carries her out, managing to pick up her bags on the way. RON is forlorn and starts to close the door just as CHRIS returns, still in Steinberg's arms.*)

RON. (*Immensely relieved.*) Boy, you really had me going there for a minute!

(CHRIS puts her hand to her mouth and kisses the mezzuzzeh, then is taken away by the rabbi. Sadly RON closes the door and goes back to the dining area.)

MRS. GOLDMAN. *(Sighs, glances at her watch.)* I'm sorry, Ronnie but I—Arthur is waiting for me ... Are you going to be all right?

RON. *(False bravado.)* I'm fine ... There's only one problem I have to deal with now.

MRS. GOLDMAN. What's that, honey?

RON. She forgot to tell me which dishes are the milky dicky and which are the fleshy dicky.

MRS. GOLDMAN. Still making jokes to cover the pain inside. Oh, baby, I can't leave you alone feeling the way you do—I'll call Arthur and we'll postpone the wedding.

RON. *(Kisses her.)* Thanks, Mom, but you go ahead. I've got to do a lot of thinking about what to do with the rest of my life.

MRS. GOLDMAN. Okay, you stay here and do whatever makes you happy. Or miserable, it's the same thing.

RON. *(Suddenly vitalized.)* No! It's not the same thing! Not any more it isn't! And if it still is, I don't want it to be! *(Heading for door.)* I'm so damn sick of being sick.

MRS. GOLDMAN. Where are you going?

RON. To get married! This has been the loneliest sixty seconds I ever spent in my life!

(HE opens the door and there is CHRIS in STEINBERG'S arms, poised to kiss the mezzuzzeh.)

RON. I was just going after you!

CHRIS. Hold it, buster. Don't get any ideas. We only came back to call me a taxi. With my leg, we couldn't figure out a way to get me on the back seat of his goddam motorcycle. (*To Steinberg.*) Oops! Sorry abut that language, Rabbi.

STEINBERG. That's nothing! Wait till you learn some *real* Jewish words! We have some beauties that can't be TOUCHED in English!

CHRIS. That's my phone over there.

(*Steinberg starts to cross with her.*)

RON. Chris, listen to me. I just got a one minute flash of what my life would be like without you. And I want to make a great big change right now.

MRS. GOLDMAN. (*Happily.*) I'll call the doctor tomorrow and tell him they gave me the right baby after all.

RON. So now, I'm going to ask you something I should have asked a long time ago. I'll even get down on bended knee for you.

(*Gets down on bended knee. CHRIS is still being carried by STEINBERG.*)

RON. (*Asides to Steinberg.*) Would you mind lowering her a bit?

(*CHRIS nods to Steinberg to do so.*)

RON. Will you marry me?

CHRIS. A minute ago you weren't sure. How can you change your mind just like that?

RON. This isn't any snap decision. I've been toying with the idea for some time!

CHRIS. Getting married isn't the kind of idea you TOY with! Living together without being married is the kind of idea you TOY with! You know, I've just done a little quick thinking, myself. I'm not sure if *I* want to marry *you* now.

RON. (*Referring to Steinberg.*) Don't tell me you're thinking of leaving me for another man?

CHRIS. Oh, Ron, get with it. If I left you, it wouldn't be for another MAN! It would be for another *woman:* ME!! Ron, I'm not the same girl who moved in here a year ago. In the past three months, I've learned that I deserve much more respect than I've been getting out of this so-called "relationship." If you're really serious about wanting to marry me—if I *were* to say yes, first I'd have to be sure I'll be getting my share of respect.

RON. You got it! I'll even throw in both my ex-wives share! Chris, give me one more chance, please.

CHRIS. Oh, Ron, I want so much to trust you. But I'm not sure how it would work for our children to have one parent who is Jewish and the other who isn't.

RON. But you're going to convert.

CHRIS. I meant YOU!

RON. Okay, honey, name whatever it is you want me to do.

CHRIS. All right. From now on, I want you to observe all the laws and traditions and customs right along with me.

RON. I will, I promise.

CHRIS. And I want you to go with me to Synagogue every Sabbath.

RON. I promise. Not only every Sabbath but every holiday, too.

MRS. GOLDMAN. Omigod! If your father were alive to hear that, he would drop dead again!

CHRIS. Those are just for starters. If you promise to do that for me, my answer is—

STEINBERG. Hannah! Wait! If you marry him *before* you pass your test, the rabbis will think that's the only reason you wanted to convert.

CHRIS. Ohh! Yeah ... Okay, Ron, here's the deal. I'll move in with my friend Doris, and after I finish my lessons and I convert, *then* we'll get married.

RON. (*Embraces her.*) You've got a deal. Hannah, may I offer you a ride now to Doris's house?

CHRIS. That's very sweet of you, Ron.

RON. Just trying to show a little respect.

CHRIS. Thank you—Uh, I almost forgot! (*To Steinberg.*) I talked to a nice Jewish girl for you, Jonas. She said she'd love to meet a cute young rabbi. She's never kept a kosher home but she said she'd love to take lessons from someone who really knows all the rules inside out.

STEINBERG. Oh, thank you.

CHRIS. So I told her *I* would coach her myself.

(*THEY all laugh and start out.*)

CHRIS. Oh, Ron!

(*HE stops.*)

CHRIS. Promise me you'll never worry again about the difference in our ages.

RON. I promise. What difference does a lousy twenty-five years make?

CHRIS. It's not twenty-*five* years, there's only *twenty* years difference.

RON. No, it's twenty-five. I'm going to be fifty-one.

CHRIS. I know, I can count. Believe me, there's only TWENTY years difference!

RON. But—that would make you—

CHRIS. (*Nodding.*) Now that I'm getting married, I can stop lying about my age!

(*RON reacts, then bursts into laughter as does EVERYONE else as THEY all head through the front door.*
FAST FADE.)

End of Play

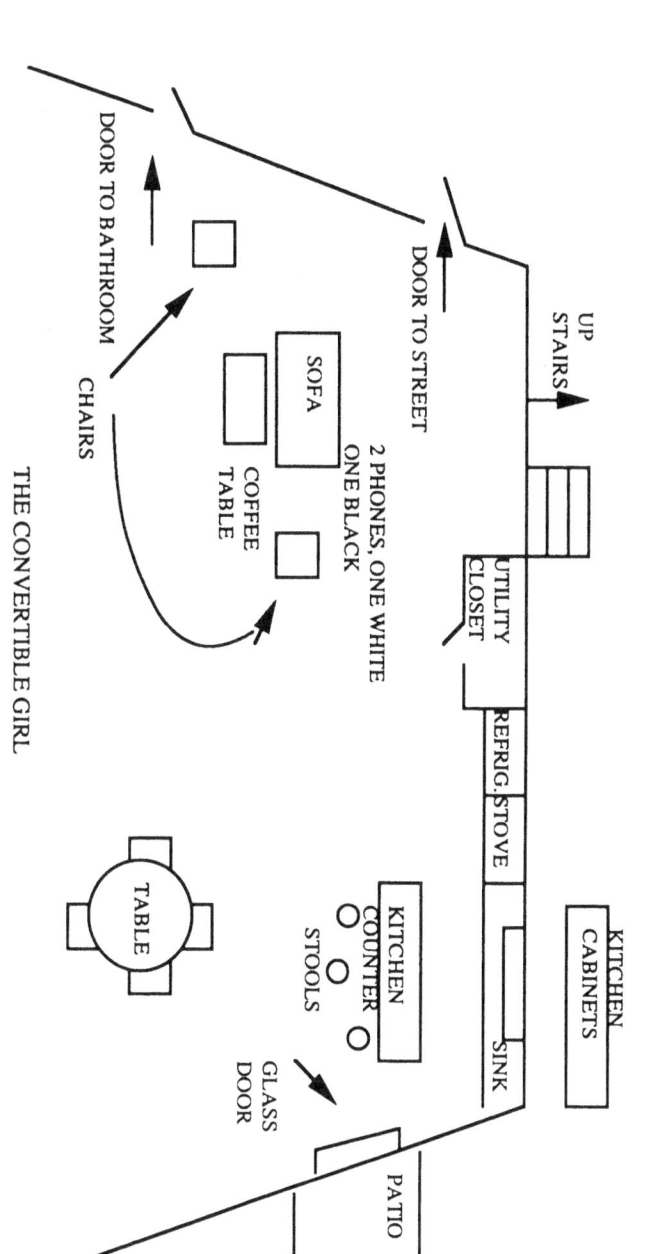

THE CONVERTIBLE GIRL

DOOR TO BATHROOM

CHAIRS

DOOR TO STREET

UP
STAIRS

SOFA

COFFEE
TABLE

2 PHONES, ONE WHITE
ONE BLACK

UTILITY
CLOSET

REFRIG. STOVE

KITCHEN
CABINETS

TABLE

KITCHEN
COUNTER

STOOLS

SINK

GLASS
DOOR

PATIO